‘When the
men were off
somewhere,
he would come
visiting their
wives more
solicitously than
any priest they’d
had before . . .’

GIOVANNI BOCCACCIO

Mrs Rosie and the Priest

Translated by
Peter Hainsworth

Contents

Andreuccio da Perugia's Neapolitan adventures

I was told some time ago about a young man from Perugia called Andreuccio, the son of a certain Pietro and a horse-dealer by trade. Having heard that horses were trading well in Naples, he put five-hundred gold florins in his bag and went off there with some other merchants, never having previously been away from home. He arrived on a Sunday evening, about vesper time, got the necessary information from his innkeeper and was in the market square early the next morning. He saw a lot of horses, many of which met with his approval, and did a good deal of bargaining without being able to agree a price for any of them. But he was keen to show that he was there to do some buying and naively and imprudently pulled out his bag of florins several times before the eyes of people coming and going past him. It was while he was negotiating, with his bag in full view, that a young Sicilian woman walked past. She was very beautiful, but ready to give any man what he wanted for a small payment. He didn't see her, but she saw his bag and immediately said to herself, 'Wouldn't I be a lucky one if that money were mine?' Then she went on her way.

There was old woman with her who was also Sicilian. As soon as she saw Andreuccio, she let the girl go on and hurried over to give him an affectionate hug. The young woman noticed and, without saying anything, stopped and waited for her on one side. Andreuccio, who had turned round and recognized the old woman, greeted her with great warmth. She promised to come and see him at his inn, but didn't keep him talking for too long just then and soon left. Andreuccio went back to his bargaining, though he made no purchases that morning. After seeing first the bag and then the intimacy with the old servant, the young woman began to wonder if she might get hold of some or all of the money. She asked a few cautious questions about who the young man was, where he was from, what he was doing there and how she came to know him. The old servant gave her all the information she wanted, almost in as much detail as Andreuccio might have supplied himself, being able to do this because she had spent a long time with his father first in Sicily and then in Perugia. She likewise told her where he was lodging and why he had come to Naples.

Once the young woman was fully informed about his family and their names, she had the basis for playing a clever trick that would bring her what she wanted. Back at her house she made sure that the old woman was busy all day so that she couldn't go and see Andreuccio. She had a much younger servant-girl to whom she had given a very good training in the sort of work she had in mind, and towards evening she sent her to the inn where Andreuccio was staying. When she arrived, she found him by chance standing alone in the doorway. She asked for Andreuccio and he said that he was the very man. At which she drew him to one side.

'Sir,' she said, 'there is a noble lady in this town who would appreciate a conversation with you, if you were so inclined.'

Andreuccio thought carefully for a moment when he heard this. He decided that he was a good-looking lad and deduced that this lady must have fallen for him, as if there were no other fine young men in Naples just then apart from himself. He quickly said that he was up for it, and asked where and when this lady wanted to have a talk with him.

The young servant-girl replied, 'She's waiting for you in her house, sir, whenever you feel like coming along.'

'Well, you lead the way and I'll follow on,' said Andreuccio immediately, with no thought of letting anyone in the inn know.

So the girl led him to the Sicilian woman's house, which was in a district called Malpertugio, a name meaning Bad Passage, which gives a clear idea of just how respectable a district it was. But Andreuccio, knowing nothing of this and quite unsuspecting, thought he was going to a most respectable house to see a lady of some standing, and confidently followed the girl into the house. As they were climbing the stairs, she called out to her mistress, 'Here's Andreuccio', and he saw her appear at the top, waiting for him.

She was still young, with a full figure and a lovely face, and her clothes and jewellery were tastefully ornate. When Andreuccio was closer, she came down three steps towards him, her arms wide, and, flinging them round his neck, stayed like that for a while without saying a word, as if too overcome to speak. Then she tearfully kissed his forehead and said in a broken voice, 'O my precious Andreuccio, welcome to my house!'

Such a heartfelt reception amazed Andreuccio, and he replied quite dazed, 'Well, it's wonderful to meet you, my lady!'

After this she took him by the hand and led him into the main room, and from there, without saying another word, into her private chamber, which was redolent with the scents of roses, orange blossom and other flowers. Andreuccio noticed a splendid curtained bed, and an abundance of beautiful dresses arranged on hangers in the south Italian way, and many other fine and costly items. In his inexperience he was fully convinced by all this that the woman could be nothing but a great lady. Once they were seated together on a chest that was at the foot of her bed, she embarked on the following speech.

'I am quite certain, Andreuccio, that you are startled at being embraced and wept over by me in this way. After all, you don't know me and and may never have heard my name mentioned. But in a moment you are going to hear something which will perhaps amaze you even more. The fact is, I am your sister. And I can tell you that, since God has granted me the enormous grace of letting me see one of my brothers before I die – though of course I want to see all of you – I shall not die unconsoled. Perhaps you have never heard a word of this. So I shall happily tell you all about it.

'As I think you may have been told, Pietro – that is, your father and mine – lived for a long time in Palermo. Thanks to his native goodness and appealing character he gained the affections of those who came to know him and still has a place in their hearts. But, among those most attached to him, there was someone who loved him more than anyone else, and that was my mother, who was a noble lady and recently widowed. She loved him so much that she put aside all fears of her father and brothers and any concern for her honour, and entered into intimate relations with him. As a result I was born into the world and am now the person you see before you.

'A little later, when a reason arose for Pietro to return to Perugia, he left me, still a very little girl, with my mother. From everything I heard, he never gave me or her another thought. If he had not been my father, I would be very critical of him, considering the ingratitude he showed to my mother – and let's leave aside the love he should have felt for me his daughter, and not by a servant-girl or some woman of easy virtue either. My mother was inspired by the truest form of love when, knowing nothing of who he was, she put herself and everything she had in his hands. But there you are. Wrongs of long ago are more easily criticized than put right.

'So he left me a little girl in Palermo. When I had grown into more or less the woman you see before you, my mother, who was a rich lady, married me to a man from Agrigento, an upstanding man of noble rank. Out of love for myself and my mother he moved to Palermo, and there, being very much on the Guelf side, he became involved in plotting with our King Charles. King Frederick got wind of the plot before any of our plans could be acted on, and so we had to flee Sicily just at the moment when I was expecting to become the finest lady there had ever been on the island. We took with us what few things we could – I mean few in comparison to all the possessions we had – and, leaving our lands and mansions behind, escaped to this city. We found King Charles very grateful. He partially compensated us for the losses we had suffered on his behalf. He gave us lands and houses, and he still gives my husband, your brother-in-law, a substantial pension, as you'll soon be able to see. So that is how I came to be here, and how, thanks to God's grace, though not at all to you, I now see you before me, my sweet brother.'

With this she clasped him to her again and kissed his forehead, still weeping tenderly.

She told her cock-and-bull story in a supremely coherent and convincing way, with not a hesitation or stutter. Andreuccio recalled that his father really had been in Palermo and he knew from his own experience what young men are like, and how prone they are to falling in love. What with the tender tears, embraces and decidedly unamorous kisses, he was convinced that what she said was more than true. When she finished, he made the following reply.

'My lady, you must not be shocked by my own amazement. To be candid, either my father for some reason of his own never spoke about you and your mother, or if he did speak of you, not a whisper reached my ears. So I had no more knowledge of you than if you had never existed. But it's all the more precious to me to have found you, my sister, in this place, because I'm here all alone and this was the thing I least expected. And to tell the truth, I can't imagine your not being precious to the grandest businessman I can think of, let alone to a small-scale merchant like myself. But please, explain one thing for me. How did you come to know I was here?'

'I was told this morning,' she replied. 'And the person who told me is a poor woman who spends a lot of time here with me, the reason being that, from what she says, she was with our father for a long time in both Palermo and Perugia. If it hadn't seemed to me more honourable for you to come here to what is your house than for me to come and see you at someone else's, I would have been with you ages ago.'

After this she started putting precise questions to him about his relatives, identifying each one by name. Andreuccio told her about them all, becoming more and more willing to believe what he should not have believed at all.

Since they kept on talking for a long time and it was very hot, she called for white wine and sweetmeats, and ensured that Andreuccio was duly served. He made to leave after this since it was now dinnertime, but she wouldn't allow it. Looking deeply distressed, she flung her arms round him, saying, 'Oh, poor me, I can tell I don't really matter to you! To think that you're here with a sister you've never seen before, in her house, where you should have come and stayed when you arrived, and you want to go off and have your dinner in an inn. No, you'll dine with me, and though my husband is not here, I'm very sorry to say, I'll do what little a lady is capable of to see you are treated with some degree of honour.'

Andreuccio could only come up with one reply.

'You do matter to me,' he said, 'as much as any sister should. But if I don't go, I shall keep them waiting for me for dinner all evening, which would be really churlish.'

'Lord in heaven,' she said, 'do you think I've nobody

in the house I can send to tell them not to expect you? Though you would be doing a finer thing, not to say your duty, if you sent a message to your friends inviting them to come and dine here. Then afterwards, if you were set on leaving, you and all the rest could go off in one big party.'

Andreuccio replied that he had no wish to see his friends that evening, and that, if this was how she felt, she should treat him as she pleased. She then made a show of sending a message to the inn telling them not to expect him for dinner. After this they talked on for a long time before sitting down to eat. They were served in a splendid fashion with a series of dishes, the woman cunningly prolonging the dinner well into the night. When they got up from the table, and Andreuccio expressed a desire to leave, she said that she could not possibly allow it. Naples was not a city for anyone to walk through at night, especially a stranger. She had sent a message to say he should not be expected for dinner and then she had sent another regarding where he was staying. He believed everything she said, and was delighted, in his deluded state, to stay on.

At her instigation conversation after dinner was prolonged and varied. Late into the night she left Andreuccio in her own chamber, with a young servant-boy to show him anything he needed, while she herself went off to another room with her maids.

It was very hot and as soon as he saw he was alone

Andreuccio removed his jacket and peeled off his leggings, which he left over the bedhead. Feeling nature calling him to lighten his stomach of the excess weight within it, he asked the servant where one did that sort of thing. The boy pointed to a door in a corner of the room.

'Go in there,' he said.

Andreuccio went insouciantly though the door. By chance he brought one of his feet down on a board, the other end of which was no longer attached to the joist on which it was resting. The result was that the board swung up in the air and then crashed downwards, taking Andreuccio with it. God was kind to him and he did himself no harm in the tumble, although he fell from a considerable height, but he was thoroughly covered in the horrible filth that the place was full of. To explain the arrangement in order to give you a clearer picture of what I've just said and what follows, two narrow beams had been fixed over the sort of narrow alleyway we often see separating two houses, with some boards nailed to them and a place to sit on fitted. It was one of these boards which had fallen with Andreuccio.

When he found himself down below in the alleyway, he was extremely upset at what had happened and began calling out to the boy. But, as soon as he had heard him fall, the boy had rushed to tell his mistress. She in her turn rushed into the bedroom, quickly looked to see if his clothes were there and found them. With them was the money, which, crazily, the ever suspicious Andreuccio always carried on his person. The Palermo tart, who now had what she had schemed for by turning into the sister of the visitor from Perugia, couldn't care less any more about Andreuccio. She went promptly over to the door which Andreuccio had passed through when he fell, and closed it.

When the boy didn't reply, Andreuccio started calling more loudly, but to no avail. He was now becoming suspicious and beginning, somewhat late in the day, to have an inkling of the trickery. He climbed on to the low wall separating the alleyway from the street and, once down on the other side, found his way to the door of the house, which he easily recognized. He stood there for a long time, vainly calling out and shaking and banging on the door. He could now see the full extent of his misfortune quite clearly, which reduced him to tears.

'Oh, poor me,' he began saying. 'How little time it's taken for me to lose five-hundred florins and a sister too!'

After a lot more of this he began again beating on the door and calling out. The result was that many people living nearby woke up and then, when the din became unbearable, got themselves out of bed. One of the lady's female servants appeared at a window, looking all sleepy, and called out in an irritated voice, 'Who's banging away down there?'

'Oh, don't you know me?' said Andreuccio. 'I'm Andreuccio, the brother of Lady Fiordiliso.'

The servant replied, 'My good man, if you've had too

much to drink, go and sleep it off and come back in the morning. I don't know anything about any Andreuccio or anything else you're gabbling on about. Do us a favour, please go away and let us get some sleep.'

'What?' said Andreuccio. 'Don't you really know what I'm saying? Oh, you must do. But if family relations in Sicily are like that and get forgotten as quickly as this, at least let me have back the clothes I left with you and I'll be glad to go on my way with only the Lord for company.'

The servant almost broke out laughing.

'Good man,' she said, 'I think you're dreaming.'

And even before she finished speaking, she was back inside with the window shut.

Andreuccio was now fully aware of his losses and the pain of the realization made him so angry it almost drove him wild. He could not recover what he had lost through words and he resorted to physical violence. He picked up a big stone and began savagely beating at the door again, only now with much more force. At this many of the neighbours who had been woken up and were out of their beds started thinking that he was some no-gooder who was inventing the whole palaver to bother the good woman. When the banging got too much for them, they started calling out from their windows, as if they were the neighbourhood dogs barking all together at some stray intruder.

'It's an outrage,' they said, 'coming at this hour of night to respectable women's houses with all this claptrap. Oh, go away, for God's sake, and please let us sleep. If you have anything to sort out with her, you can come back tomorrow. Just don't be such a blasted nuisance tonight.'

What they were saying perhaps encouraged the good Sicilian woman's pimp, who was inside the house, though he had not been seen or heard till now by Andreuccio. He came to the window and in his best horrible and savage voice called out loudly, 'Who's that down there?'

Andreuccio looked up when he heard this and saw someone who, so far as he could tell (which was not much), had the air of a man to be taken seriously. He had a thick black beard and was yawning and rubbing his eyes, as if he'd just awoken from deep sleep.

'I'm a brother of the lady of the house,' replied Andreuccio nervously.

The man did not wait for him to go on.

'I can't think,' he said in an even more intimidating voice than before, 'why I'm stopping myself from coming down there and giving you such a thrashing you won't ever move again. An irritating drunk of a donkey, that's what you must be, not letting anyone round here get any sleep tonight.'

With that he turned back inside and bolted the window.

Some of the neighbours knew what sort of a man he

was and whispered a few fearful words of advice to Andreuccio.

'For God's sake,' they said, 'go away, good man, don't get yourself murdered down there. Go away for your own good.'

Being already terrified by the ruffian's voice and appearance, Andreuccio saw every reason for accepting this advice, which he felt was motivated by simple goodwill. He was now as dejected as anyone could be and despaired of recovering his money. He set off towards the part of the city he had come from following the servant-girl earlier that day, aiming to get back to his inn, but with no idea of the way. Then, since the stench he could smell coming from him was disgusting, he decided to go towards the sea in order to wash himself down. But he turned leftwards and headed up a street called the Ruga Catalana, or Catalan Way. This was taking him to the higher part of the city, when he happened to see in front two figures coming towards him with a lantern. He was afraid they might be part of the official watch, or else just up to no good. He noticed an open building nearby and quietly crept in to try to avoid them. But it was as if they had been directed precisely to that spot. They too entered the building. One was carrying various tools round his neck, which he unloaded, and the two of them began looking the tools over and commenting on them.

At a certain point in their conversation, one of them said, 'What can it be? I can smell the worst stink I've ever smelt.' And then, lifting up the lantern a bit, they saw the miserable Andreuccio.

'Who's that there?' they asked, astounded.

When Andreuccio said nothing, they came over to him with the light and asked him what he was doing there in such a repulsive state. Andreuccio told them the whole story of what had happened to him. They guessed where it could have been and said to each other, 'It must have all happened at that villain Buttafuoco's.'

'My good lad,' said one of them, turning to Andreuccio, 'you might have lost your money, but you have plenty reason for praising the Lord that you happened to have that fall and then couldn't get back into the house. If you hadn't fallen, you can be sure that you'd have been murdered as soon as you dropped off to sleep, and then you'd have lost your life as well as your money. But what's the point of crying over it at this stage? You've as much chance of getting a penny back as of picking stars from the sky. You're likely to end up dead if that villain hears you've been blabbing away.'

Then, after some conferring together, they put a proposal to him.

'Look, we feel sorry for you,' they said. 'So, if you want to join us in a certain project we are en route to perform, we are of the definite opinion that your share of the profits will amount to much more than what you have lost.'

Andreuccio, in his desperate state, replied that he was ready and willing.

That day had seen the burial of a certain Archbishop of Naples called Messer Filippo Minutolo. He had been buried in elaborate finery with a ruby ring on his finger worth over five-hundred gold florins. The two of them had in mind to detach it. They explained the scheme to Andreuccio, who let greed override good sense, and the three of them set off.

Andreuccio was still giving off a strong smell as they proceeded towards the cathedral.

'Can't we find a way,' said one of the two at a certain point, 'for this companion of ours to have a wash somewhere to stop him stinking so horribly?'

'Yes,' said the other, 'we're near to a well now. It's always had a pulley and a big bucket. Let's go over and give him a quick wash.'

When they reached the well, they found the rope was there but the bucket had been removed. So they decided to tie Andreuccio to the rope and lower him into the well. Once at the bottom, he would wash himself, and then, when he had done, he would give the rope a shake and they would pull him up.

So they moved into action and lowered Andreuccio into the well. But it so happened that some of the night watch were feeling thirsty because of the heat and also because they had been chasing after someone. They were coming towards the well to get a drink when the other two saw them, and at once took to their heels, without any of the company coming after water seeing them.

Down in the well, Andreuccio, having finished washing, shook the rope a few times. The thirsty watchmen, who had now unstrapped their bucklers, their weapons and their surcoats, began pulling on the rope, believing that it was attached to a big bucketful of water.

As soon as Andreuccio saw he was near the rim of the well, he let go of the rope and grabbed hold of the rim in his hands. The sight was enough to terrify the watchmen, who immediately, without a word, let go of the rope and ran off as fast as they could. Andreuccio was profoundly startled. If he had not kept a firm hold, he would have fallen back into the well and perhaps have hurt himself badly, or even finished up dead. Once he was finally out of the well, he found the abandoned weaponry, which he knew his companions had not been carrying, and was even more amazed. Nervous, unclear what was going on, bemoaning his misfortune, he decided to take himself off without touching anything and wandered away with no idea of where he was heading. He was going along like this when he bumped into his two companions, who were coming back to pull him up out of the well. They were astonished and asked him who had actually done that. Andreuccio replied that he did not know, but gave them a full account of what had occurred and of what he had found by the well.

His companions realized what had happened and explained, laughing, why they had run away and who the people were who had pulled him up. Then, without wasting any more words since it was already midnight, they all went off to the cathedral. They got in quite easily and reached the tomb, which was marble and very large. They used their irons to lift the cover, which was enormously heavy, raising it just enough for a single man to get inside, and then they propped it up.

When this was done, one of them asked, 'Who's going to go inside?'

'Not me,' said the other.

'Nor me either,' said the first. 'But let Andreuccio go in.'

'I'm not doing that,' said Andreuccio.

Both of them turned on him.

'What do you mean you won't go in?' they said. 'By God, if you don't go in, we'll give you a bashing round the head with one of these iron poles and that'll be the end of you.'

This put the wind up Andreuccio. He went inside, thinking to himself as he did so, 'These two are making me enter the tomb in order to trick me. When I've passed them everything and am getting myself out again, they'll be off and I'll be left with nothing.'

He decided first and foremost to pocket his own share. He remembered the precious ring he had heard them discussing and, as soon as he was in the tomb, he took it off the Archbishop's finger and put it on his own. Then he passed them the crozier, the mitre and the gloves and stripped the body down to the shirt, passing them each item, saying that was all there was. They protested that the ring must be somewhere and told him to look everywhere. He replied that he couldn't find it and pretended to go on looking, keeping them waiting for some time. But they were as canny as he was. They continued telling him to keep looking and then, picking their moment, they pulled away the prop supporting the lid of the tomb and ran off, leaving Andreuccio enclosed within. Anyone can guess how Andreuccio felt when he heard the lid fall.

He tried many times to push up the lid with his head and shoulders, but his efforts were useless. He was so overcome with the anguish of it all that he passed out, collapsing on the Archbishop's dead body. And anyone who had seen the two of them would have had difficulty deciding which was the more lifeless, the Archbishop or Andreuccio. When he came to his senses, he broke into a flood of tears, foreseeing that he could not avoid one of two ends. If no one came to open the tomb, he was doomed to die of hunger and the stink among the worms from the corpse. Or else, if people came and found him inside the tomb, he would be hung as a thief.

With these bleakly distressing thoughts going round in his head, he heard movement in the church and many people talking. They were, he gathered, going to do what he and his companions had already done. This sharply increased his terror. But when they had opened the tomb and propped up the lid, they began to argue about who should go inside, which none of them wanted to do. At last, after much dispute, a priest said, 'What are you frightened of? Do you think he's going to eat you? The dead don't eat people. I'll be the one to go in.' With this he leaned over the edge of the tomb, turned his head outwards and swung his legs inside in order to lower himself down. Andreuccio saw what was going on, jumped up and seized the priest by one of his legs and made as if to pull him down inside. When the priest felt himself being pulled, he let out an enormous shriek and scrambled out of the tomb as fast as he could. This terrified the rest of them. Leaving the tomb open, they took off as if they were being chased by a hundred thousand devils.

Seeing them go, Andreuccio clambered out of the tomb, happier than he could have hoped, and left the church by the way he had come in. It was almost daylight as he walked off, trusting to luck, with the ring on his finger. But he reached the seafront and finished up somehow at his inn, where he discovered that the merchants he had come with and the innkeeper had been worrying about him all night. He told them what had happened to him and they all opined that he should take the innkeeper's advice and leave Naples immediately. He quickly did so and returned to Perugia, with his funds now invested in a ring, after having set out to do some horse-trading.

Ricciardo da Chinzica loses his wife

There was once a judge in Pisa with more brains than muscle called Messer Ricciardo da Chinzica, who may have thought that what worked well with his studies would satisfy a wife too. Being very rich, he was able to devote considerable time and effort to searching for a good-looking young lady to marry, whereas, if he had been able to give himself the sort of professional counsel he gave to others, good looks and youth were just what he should have run away from. And he managed it: Ser Lotto Gualandi gave him one of his daughters in marriage. She was called Bartolommea and she was one of the best-looking and most fanciable girls in Pisa, though admittedly there aren't many there who don't look like hairy spiders. The judge took her home with great razzmatazz, and the marriage-feast was magnificent.

When he finally geared himself up for the actual consummation, he just about brought it off. But being scrawny, wizened and not exactly spunky, next morning he had to have a glass of fortified wine, some sweet biscuits and other pick-me-ups before he could re-enter the world of the living. The experience gave the judge a better idea of his capabilities than he had had before, and he began teaching his wife a calendar of saints' days of the kind that schoolboys pore over looking for holidays which might have been made in Ravenna. As he now showed her, there wasn't a day that wasn't a saint's day, or rather every day had a multitude of them. Reverence for these demanded, as he demonstrated on various grounds, that man and woman should abstain from acts of congress. Then he threw in fasts, the four Ember days, evening vigils for the Apostles and hundreds of other saints, Fridays, Saturdays, the Lord's Day, the whole of Lent, certain phases of the moon and endless other special cases, no doubt assuming that the breaks from court-work he enjoyed from time to time applied just as much to women in bed. So this was how he managed things for a long time, with his wife becoming seriously depressed from being given at best a monthly treat, while he always kept a watchful eye on her just in case someone else gave her lessons about working days like the ones he had given her about saints' days.

Since the next summer was very hot, Messer Ricciardo found himself wanting to go off to a beautiful property he had near Monte Nero, where he could relax and enjoy the air for a few days. With him he took his lovely wife. To give her some entertainment while they were there, one day he organized a fishing trip. The two of them sailed out on small boats to watch the spectacle, he on one with the fishermen, she on the other with some ladies. They were so captivated that they drifted several miles along the coast almost without realizing it. But while they were gazing in rapt attention, a sloop suddenly came on the scene, belonging to Paganino da Mare, a celebrated corsair of the time. Once it sighted the boats, it set a course straight for them. They were unable to get away fast enough and Paganino caught up with the boat with the ladies in it. As soon as he laid eyes on Messer Ricciardo's beautiful wife, he stopped wanting any other booty, and whisked her into his sloop under the eyes of her husband, who was now on shore, and sailed away.

It doesn't take much to imagine how upset the judge was by the sight, given that he was so jealous he was fearful of the very air she breathed. In Pisa and elsewhere, he started fruitlessly complaining about the criminal behaviour of corsairs, but without discovering who had carried off his wife, or where they had taken her.

When Paganino took in how beautiful she was, he felt that he was on to a good thing. Not having a wife, he thought he might hang on to her permanently and began gently soothing her tears, which were copious. He had long ago thrown away saints' calendars and forgotten all about feast-days and holidays. That night he consoled her with some action, on the grounds that words had not helped much during the day. His consolations were so effective that the judge and his rules had gone entirely out of her head before they reached Monaco, and she began to have the time of her life with Paganino. And once he had got her there, he not only consoled her day and night, but honoured her as his wife.

After a while Messer Ricciardo got wind of the whereabouts of his good lady. Ardently desiring to do something and believing that no one else could manage to do what needed to be done, he made up his mind to go and get her himself, being prepared to pay out any amount of money to recover her. So he set to sea and sailed to Monaco. Once there he caught sight of his wife, and she caught sight of him, as she reported back to Paganino that evening, also informing him what his intentions were. When Messer Ricciardo saw Paganino the next morning, he went up to him and quickly started an easy, friendly conversation with him, while Paganino pretended all the while not to recognize him and waited for him to get to the point. When he judged the moment had arrived, deploying his best abilities in the most ingratiating way possible, Messer Ricciardo disclosed the reason why he had come to Monaco, begging Paganino to take as much money as he wanted and give him back the lady.

'Sir,' replied Paganino with a cheerful expression on his face, 'you are very welcome here. My reply in brief is as follows: it is true I have a young woman in my house, though I don't know whether she's your wife or someone else's. I don't know anything about her except what I've gathered from her during her stay with me. If you are her husband as you say, I'll take you to her since you seem to me a likeable gentleman and I'm sure she'll recognize you very well. If she says that the situation is as you say and wishes to go away with you, then, since I do love a likeable man such as you, you can give me the amount you yourself decide on for a ransom. But if the situation should be different, it would be indecent for you to try to take her from me, since I've got youth on my side and can hold a woman in my arms as well as any man, particularly one who is more attractive than any other girl I've ever seen.'

'She certainly is my wife,' said Messer Ricciardo, 'as you'll soon see if you take me to where she is. She'll fling her arms round my neck straight away. So I won't ask for the terms to be different from those you've thought up yourself.'

'Let's go then,' said Paganino.

So they walked off to Paganino's house and went into a reception-room, from where Paganino sent for her. She appeared from a chamber properly and neatly dressed and went over where Messer Ricciardo was waiting with Paganino. There she addressed only the sort of remarks to Messer Ricciardo that she might have made to any other stranger who had come with Paganino to his house. The judge, who was expecting to be given a rapturous welcome, was amazed.

'Could it be,' he began to wonder, 'that depression and my protracted sufferings ever since I lost her have altered me so much that she doesn't recognize me?'

'Lady,' he said, 'taking you fishing has cost me dear. No one has suffered as much as I have since I lost you, and here you are seeming not to recognize me, given the unfriendly way you're talking. Can't you see that I'm your Messer Ricciardo, who's come here to pay whatever sum is demanded by this fine gentleman in whose house we find ourselves, so that I can have you back and take you away from here? He's being kind enough to restore you to me for a sum of my own choosing.'

The lady turned to him and gave him a faint smile.

'Are you addressing me, sir?' she asked. 'You should check you've not mistaken me for somebody else. As far as I'm concerned, I don't recall ever seeing you before.'

'It's you who should check what you're saying,' said Messer Ricciardo. 'Look at me properly. If you're willing to do a little serious recalling, you're bound to see that I'm your very own Ricciardo da Chinzica.'

'Sir, you'll forgive me,' said the lady, 'but it's not as right and proper as you imagine for me to give you a lengthy looking-over. All the same, I've looked at you enough to know that I've never seen you before.'

Messer Ricciardo imagined that she was acting in this way out of fear of Paganino and did not want to admit to knowing him in his presence. So, after a few moments, he asked Paganino if he would be so kind as to let him speak with the lady alone in her chamber. Paganino said that he was happy to do so, on condition that he didn't start kissing her against her will. Then he told the lady to go with him into the chamber, listen to what he wanted to say and give him whatever reply she felt like.

Once the lady and Messer Ricciardo were in the chamber by themselves and had sat down, Messer Ricciardo began entreating her. 'Oh, heart of my life, my own sweet soul, my one hope, don't you recognize your Ricciardo, who loves you more than he loves himself? How can it be? Have I altered so much? Oh, lovely darling girl, at least give me a little look.'

The lady broke out laughing and wouldn't let him go on. 'You are very well aware,' she said, 'that I've not such a bad memory that I don't know you are Messer Ricciardo da Chinzica, my husband. But you made a poor show of knowing me as long as I was with you. You're not as wise as you want people to think you are, and you never were. If you had been, you really should have had the wit to see that I was young, fresh and frisky, and then have consequently acknowledged that young ladies require something else apart from food and clothing, though modesty forbids them to spell it out. But you know how you managed all that.

'You shouldn't have married, if you liked studying law more than studying your wife. Not that I thought you were much of a judge. You seemed more like a crier calling out holy days and feast-days, you knew them so well, not to mention fast-days and overnight vigils. Let me tell you that if you had given as many days off to the labourers working your lands as you did to the one who should have been working my little plot, you'd not have harvested one grain of corn. By chance I've met with this man here, chosen by God, because he shows a compassionate concern for my young age. And I stay with him in this chamber, where no one knows what a feast-day is. I mean those feast-days that you celebrated one after another, piously serving the Lord in preference to the ladies. Saturdays don't pass through that door, neither do Fridays, vigils, Ember days or Lent, which just goes on and on. No, it's all work, day and night, banging away all the time. As soon as the bell rang for matins this morning, there we were back at it, doing the same job again and again, as I know very well. So I intend to stay and work with him while I'm young, and keep feast-days and penances and fasts for when I'm old. Get out of here as soon as you can and good luck to you. Go and keep your saints' days as much as you like without me.'

Messer Ricciardo's distress at hearing her speak like this was unbearable.

'Oh, sweet soul of mine,' he said, when he realized she had finished, 'what are you saying? Aren't you bothered at all about your family's honour or your own? Do you want to stay here as this fellow's tart, living in mortal sin, rather than be my wife in Pisa? He'll get fed up with you and throw you out in total disgrace. But I'll always hold you dear and you'll always be the lawful mistress of my house, even if I didn't want to be your husband. Oh, please listen. Are you going to let this unbridled, immoral lust make you forget your honour and forget me, when I love you more than my very life? Please, my dear love, don't say things like that any more, just come away with me. Now that I know what you want, I'll really make an effort from now on. So, sweetheart, change your mind, come away with me. I've been so miserable since you were carried off.'

'Now that there's nothing to be done about it,' said the lady, 'I don't see how anyone apart from me can be squeamish over my honour. I just wish my family had been a bit more squeamish when they gave me to you! But since they didn't bother about my honour then, I don't intend to bother about theirs now. If my sin's a mortar one, I'll stay stuck in it like a pestle. So don't you worry about me. And what's more, let me tell you that I feel like Paganino's wife here, while I felt like your tart in Pisa, what with lunar charts and geometric squarings having to align your planet and mine, while here Paganino has me in his arms all night, squeezing me, biting me, and the state he leaves me in God alone can tell you. Then you say you'll make an effort. Doing what? Waiting for something to happen? Straightening it by hand? I can tell you've turned into a redoutable knight since I saw you last! Go on, do your best to come to life. But you can't manage it. I don't think you belong in this world, you look such a wasted, miserable little wimp. And another thing. If he leaves me – which I don't think he's inclined to do as long I want to stay with him – I've no intention of ever coming back to you. Squeeze you till you squeaked, and you still wouldn't produce a spoonful of sauce. That meant that when I was with you I just lost out and paid out. I'm after better returns somewhere else. To go back to where I started, I tell you there are no feast-days and no vigils here, where I intend to stay. So leave as quickly as you can, and the Lord be with you. If you don't, I'll start shouting that you're forcing yourself on me.'

Messer Ricciardo saw that the game was up, recognizing there and then the folly in marrying a young wife without the appropriate wherewithal. He left the chamber in a saddened, suffering state and spoke a lot of waffle to Paganino, which got him nowhere. In the end, he left the lady and returned empty-handed to Pisa. The blow affected his mind and, when he was walking around the city, if someone greeted him or asked him a question, he would only reply, 'A horrid hole hates a holy day.'

It wasn't long before he died. When Paganino heard, knowing how much the lady loved him, he took her as his lawful wedded wife. Thereafter, with no thought for holy days or vigils or Lent, they worked their patch as much as their limbs would let them, and had a wonderful time together.

Mrs Rosie and the Priest

So, to begin, there's a village not far from here called Varlungo, as every one of you knows or will have heard from other people. It had once a valiant priest, a fine figure of a man who served the ladies well. He was not much of a reader, but every Sunday he would spout wholesome holy verbiage beneath the churchyard elm to refresh the spirits of his parishioners. When the men were off somewhere, he would come visiting their wives more solicitously than any priest they'd had before, sometimes bringing religious bits and pieces, holy water or candle-ends into their houses, and giving them his blessing.

Now among the women of the parish he took a fancy to, there was one he particularly liked, called Mrs Rosie Hues. She was the wife of a labourer by the name of Willy Welcome, and she really was a lovely ripe country-girl, tanned, sturdy, with lots of grinding potential. She was also better than any girl around at playing the tambourine, singing songs like 'The water's running down my river', and dancing reels and jigs, when she had to, waving a pretty little kerchief in her hand. With all these talents, she reduced the good priest to a quivering wreck. He would wander round the village all day trying to catch sight of her. When he realized she was in church on a Sunday morning, he would launch into a Kyrie or a Sanctus and struggle to come over as a virtuoso singer, though he sounded more like an ass braying, whereas, when he didn't see her there, he barely bothered to sing at all. All the same, he was clever enough not to arouse the suspicions of Willy Welcome or any neighbours of his.

From time to time, he would send Mrs Rosie presents in an effort to win her over. Sometimes it was a bunch of fresh garlic, since he grew the best in the region in a vegetable garden he worked with his own hands, sometimes it was a basket of berries, and now and then a bunch of shallots or spring onions. When he saw his chance, he would give her a hurt look and mutter a few gentle reproaches, while she acted cold, pretending not to notice, and looking all supercilious. So the estimable priest was left getting nowhere.

Now it happened one day that the priest was kicking his heels in the noontime heat out in the countryside with nothing much to do, when he bumped into Willy Welcome driving an ass loaded up with a pile of things on its back. He greeted him and asked him where he was going.

'To tell the truth, Father sir,' replied Willy, 'I'm off to town on a bit of business. I'm transporting these materials to Mr Notary Bonaccorri da Ginestreto to get him to aid and assist with a fiddle-faddle on the legal side that the assessor is officializing to put the whole house in order at last.'

'That, my son, is a good thing to do,' said the priest, full of glee. 'Go with my blessing and come back soon. And if you should happen to see Lapuccio or Naldino, don't let it slip your mind to tell them to bring me those straps for my threshing flails.'

Willy said he would do that and went off towards Florence, while the priest decided the time had come for him to go and try his luck with Rosie. He strode out vigorously and did not stop until he reached her house. He went in, calling out, 'God be with us! Is anyone here?'

Rosie was up at the top of the house. Hearing him, she shouted, 'Father, you're very welcome. What are you doing all fancy free in this heat?'

'God help me,' said the priest, ' I've come to spend a little time with you, having just met your man on his way to town.'

Rosie was downstairs by now. She sat and began cleaning some cabbage seeds her husband had sifted out a short time before.

'Well, Rosie,' said the priest, 'must you go on being the death of me like this?'

Rosie began to laugh.

'Well, what am I doing to you?' she said.

'You're not doing anything to me,' said the priest, 'but you don't let me do what I'd like to do to you, which is love my neighbour as God commanded.'

'Oh, get on with you,' said Rosie. 'Do priests do things of that sort?'

'Yes,' said the priest, 'and better than other men. And why shouldn't we? I tell you, we do a much, much better job. And do you know why? It's because we let the pond fill up before the mill starts grinding. And truly I can give you just what you need, if you'll only stay quiet and let me do the business.'

'What do you mean, just what I need?' said Rosie. 'You priests are all tighter-fisted than the devil himself.'

'I don't know,' said the priest. 'Just ask me. Maybe you want a nice little pair of shoes, or a headscarf, or a pretty woollen waistband, or maybe something else.'

'That's all very well, Brother Priest,' said Rosie. 'I've enough of that stuff. But if you're that keen on me, you can do me a particular favour, and then I'll do what you want.'

'Tell me what you're after and I'll be glad to do it,' said the priest.

'I have to go to Florence on Saturday,' said Rosie, 'to give in the wool I've been spinning and get my spinning wheel mended. If you let me have five pounds (which I know you've got), I'll get the pawnbroker to give me back my purple skirt and the decorated Sunday belt I wore when I got married. You know not having it has meant I can't go to church or anywhere respectable. And after that I'll be up for what you want for evermore.'

'God help me,' said the priest, 'I haven't the money on

me. But trust me, I'll make sure you have it before Saturday.'

'Oh yes,' said Rosie, 'you're all great at making promises. And then you don't keep any of them. Do you think you can treat me the way you treated Nell the Belle, who was left with just a big bass tum to play with? You're not going to do the same to me, by God. She ended up on the game because of you. If you haven't got it here, go and get it.'

'Oh, please,' said the priest, 'don't make me go all the way back to the house. You can tell my luck is up, and there's no one about. It could be that when I came back someone would be here to get in our way. I don't know when it might next stand up as well as it's standing up now.'

'That's all very fine,' she said, 'but if you're willing to go, go. If not, you'll just have to manage.'

He saw that she was only going to agree to his wishes when a contract was signed and delivered, whereas he was hoping for a bit of free access.

'Look,' he said, 'you don't believe I'll bring you the money. What about if I leave you this blue cape of mine as a guarantee? It's a good one.'

Rosie gave him a haughty look.

'This cape,' she said, 'how much is it worth?'

'What do you mean, how much is it worth?' said the priest. 'Let me tell you it's Douai cloth, double ply, maybe triple ply, and there are even people here who say it's got some foreply in it. I paid seven pounds at Lotto's second-hand clothes shop less than two weeks ago. It had five shillings knocked off, so it was a bargain, according to Bulietto d'Alberto, who you know is a bit of an expert in blue cloths.'

'Oh yes?' said Rosie. 'God help me, I'd never have believed it. But give it to me first.'

The good priest, who was feeling hard-pressed by his loaded weapon, unfastened his cape and passed it over.

'Well, Mr Priest,' she said, when she'd put it away, 'let's go down here to the shed. It doesn't get visitors.'

So off they went. And there he covered her in the sloppiest kisses in the world, introduced her to God's holy bliss and enjoyed himself generally with her for a good while. He finally left in the uncaped state priests normally appear in only at weddings and went back to the church.

There he reflected how all the candle-ends he picked up from his parishioners in the course of a year weren't worth half a fiver, and felt he had made a mistake. Now regretting leaving the cape behind, he started thinking about how to get it back at no cost to himself. Since he was quite crafty-minded, he figured out a good way of doing so. And it worked.

The next day being a feast-day, he sent the son of a neighbour of his to Rosie Hues's house, with a request for her to be so kind as to lend him her stone mortar, since Binguccio del Poggio and Nuto Buglietti were dining with him that morning and he wanted to make a sauce. Rosie sent it back with the boy. When it got to round lunchtime, the priest guessed Willy Welcome and Rosie Hues would be eating. He called his curate and said to him, 'Pick up that mortar and take it back to Mrs Rosie. Tell her, "The Father is immensely grateful and would like to have back the cape the boy left with you as a guarantee." '

The curate went to Rosie's house with the mortar and found her with Willy at the table eating their meal. He set down the mortar and gave them the priest's message.

Rosie was all set to give her reply to this request for the cape. But Willy's brow darkened.

'So you need guarantees from our estimated father, do you?' he said. 'I swear to Christ, I could really give you a clout up the bracket. Go and fetch it right now, and get yourself cancered while you're at it. And watch out for him wanting anything else of ours. He'd better not be told no, whatever it is. Even if it's our donkey, our donkey he gets.'

Rosie got up grumbling to herself and went over to the linen-chest. She took out the cape and passed it to the curate.

'You must give that priest a message from me,' she said, 'Say, "Rosie Hues vows to God that you'll never again be sauce-pounding in her mortar. That last time you didn't do yourself any credit." '

The curate went off with the cape and relayed Rosie's message to the priest, who burst out laughing.

'You can tell her next time you see her,' he told him, 'that if she won't lend out the mortar, I won't lend her the pestle. The one goes with the other.'

Willy believed that his wife had spoken as she did because he had told her off and gave the matter no further thought. But coming off worst made Rosie fall out with the priest, and she refused to speak to him until the grape-harvest, when he terrified her by threatening to have her stuffed into the mouth of the biggest devil in hell. She made her peace with him over fermenting must and roasting chestnuts, and after that the two of them had a good guzzle together on various occasions. To make up for the five pounds, the priest had her tambourine re-covered and a dinky little bell attached, which made her very happy.

Patient Griselda

Years ago a young man called Gualtieri inherited the marquisate of Saluzzo as the eldest son of the family. Being unmarried and childless, he spent all his time hunting birds and beasts, without giving a thought to marriage or future offspring. He should have been considered a very wise man, but his subjects disapproved. They kept begging him to get himself a wife so that he should not die without an heir and they should not be left without a lord. They kept offering to find him one with a suitable father and mother, who would satisfy their hopes and who would make him very happy.

Gualtieri's response was as follows: 'My friends, you are forcing me into something I had been completely set on never ever doing, given how difficult it is to find someone with the right character and habits, how plentiful are the inappropriate candidates, and how hard life becomes for the man who ends up with someone he doesn't get on with. You claim you can tell the daughters' characters from how the fathers and mothers behave, and argue on that basis that you can provide me with a wife I'll be pleased with. That is rubbish. I don't see how you can know the fathers properly, or the mothers' secrets for that matter. Besides, even if you could, daughters are very often unlike their fathers and their mothers. But since you like the idea of tying me up in these chains, I'll try to satisfy you, and, in order not to end up blaming anyone but myself if things should go wrong, I want to do the finding myself. But I tell you that if you don't honour and respect whoever I choose, you'll learn to your cost how hard it's been for me to take a wife against my will, just because you begged me to.'

His valiant subjects replied that they would be happy just so long as he could bring himself to get married.

Gualtieri had been impressed for a good while by the behaviour of a poverty-stricken young woman from a village near his family home. Since he also judged her to be beautiful, he calculated that life with her could be very pleasant. He looked no further and made up his mind to marry her. He had the father summoned and entered into an agreement with this complete pauper to take the girl as his wife.

That done, he called together all his friends in the area he ruled.

'My friends,' he said to them, 'you have been eager for me to make my mind up about a wife for some time. Well, I have made a decision, more out of wanting to comply with your wishes than from any desire to be married on my part. You know what you promised me – that is, to be content with the woman I chose, whoever she was, and to honour her as your lady. The time has come when I am about to keep my promise to you, and when I expect you to keep yours to me. I have found very near here a young woman after my heart. I intend to make her my wife and to bring her into my house in a few days. So arrange for the marriage-feast to be a fine one and to give her an honourable welcome. In that way I shall be able to say I am happy with how you have fulfilled your promise, and you will be able to say the same about me.'

His trusty subjects all replied that they were happy with this and that, no matter who she was, they would treat her as their lady and would honour her as such in every way. Then they all set about organizing a suitably grand and joyous celebration. And Gualtieri did his part too, arranging for a sumptuous and splendid marriage-feast, to which he invited a multitude of friends, relations, great nobles and other people from the surrounding area. In addition he had beautiful, expensive dresses made to fit a young woman who, he judged, had the same measurements as the girl he had decided to marry. Not only that, but he ordered belts, rings and a lovely, costly tiara, plus everything else a new bride should have.

Soon after sunrise on the day appointed for the wedding, Gualtieri mounted his horse, and all those who had come to honour him did the same. Everything needed was now in order, and he called out, 'Gentlemen, it is time to go for the new bride.'

After which he set off along the road to the village with the whole company. When they reached the girl's father's cottage, they found her hurrying back from the spring with some other women in the hope of catching sight of Gualtieri's bride. When he saw her, he called out to her by her name – that is, Griselda – and asked her where her father was.

'My lord,' she replied bashfully, 'he is in the house.'

Gualtieri dismounted and, telling everyone to wait, entered the poor cottage. Inside he found the father, a man called Giannucolo, to whom he said, 'I have come to make your Griselda my wife, but first I want to learn something from her own lips in your presence.'

What he asked her was whether, when he took her as his wife, she would do everything she could to please him, would not be upset by anything he might say or do, and would be obedient, together with many other questions of this sort. She replied yes to everything. Then Gualtieri took her by the hand and led her outside, where, in the presence of his whole company and everyone else, he had her stripped naked. He ordered the clothing he had had made to be brought and immediately had her dressed, and shoes put on her, and a tiara placed on her hair, unkempt though it was. Everyone was amazed.

'Gentlemen,' he said, 'this is the person I intend should be my wife, if she wishes to have me for her husband.'

Then he turned to her, standing there bashful and

awkward, and said, 'Griselda, do you want me for your husband?'

'Yes, my lord,' she replied.

'And I want you for my wife,' he said.

With that, before everyone present, he formally married her. Then he had her set on a charger, with attendants to do her honour, and took her home. The marriage-feast was grand and fine, and the festivities no different from what they would have been if he had married the daughter of the king of France.

The young wife's character and behaviour seemed to change with her change of clothing. As I said earlier, she had a lovely face and figure. And now to her natural good looks she added enough charm, attraction and refinement to make you think she could not possibly have been Giannucolo's daughter and a shepherd-girl, but the daughter of some noble lord. Everyone who had known her before was astounded. What is more, she was so ready to obey and serve her husband that he considered himself the most contented and satisfied man in the world. She was similarly so gracious and kindly towards her husband's subjects that every one of them loved her wholeheartedly and spontaneously honoured her in every way, asking God in their prayers to give her health, prosperity and greater glory still. If they used to say that Gualtieri had acted ill-advisedly in taking such a wife, now they said he was a paragon of wisdom and insight, arguing that no one else could have perceived the exceptional virtues concealed beneath the poverty of her peasant dress. All in all, before much time had passed, she had people speaking of her good qualities and virtuous deeds throughout the marquisate and beyond, and completely turning round any negative comments about her husband that had been made when he married her.

She had not been with Gualtieri very long when she became pregnant, and in due course she gave birth to a little girl, much to Gualtieri's delight. But a little later a strange idea came into his head. He felt a need to test her patience by inflicting unbearable torments on her over a prolonged period of time. First of all he made cutting remarks, and gave an impression of being angry with her. He said that his men were badly put out by her low-class origins, all the more now that she was having children. The girl-child was a particular source of resentment, and they wouldn't stop muttering about her.

When his lady heard this, she kept her composure and gave no sign of being thrown off the virtuous course she had set herself.

'My lord,' she said, 'treat me in the way that most accords with your honour and your happiness. I shall be content with anything. I am aware I'm less than they are and that I didn't deserve the honour you have had the generosity to bestow on me.'

Her response was warmly received by Gualtieri, who recognized that any honour that he or anyone else had paid her had not made her feel in the slightest bit superior.

A little while later, after giving his wife the general impression that his subjects couldn't stand the little girl she had borne him, he had a word with one of the household staff and sent him to her. The man addressed her with a distressed air.

'My lady,' he said, 'I am obliged to do something my lord commands me to do, if I do not wish to die. He has ordered me to take this daughter of yours and . . .'

He stopped there. Hearing his words and seeing his face, the lady recalled what her husband had been saying and deduced that he had orders to kill the child. She quickly took her from her cradle, kissed her and blessed her. For all the immense pain in her heart, she again kept her composure and put the child in the man's arms.

'Take her,' she said, 'and carry out to the letter what your lord and mine has ordered you to do. Only do not leave her for animals and birds to devour, unless he told you to.'

The servant took the child away and passed on what his wife had said to Gualtieri, who was astounded by her constancy. He then sent the servant off with the child to a female relative of his in Bologna, with a request to bring her up and educate her with the utmost care, but not to let anyone know whose daughter she was.

The next thing to happen was that the lady became pregnant again. In due course she gave birth to a male child, which pleased Gualtieri immensely. But what he had done already was not enough for him. His criticisms became sharper and sharper, and one day, his face contorted with rage, he said this to her:

'My lady, ever since you had this boy child, I haven't been able to live with these men of mine. They are bitterly against some grandson of Giannucolo ending up their lord after me. If I don't want to be hounded out of here, I'm afraid I'm going to have to do what I did the other time, and then in the end I'm going to have to leave you and take another wife.'

The lady heard him out without flinching.

'My lord,' was all she replied, 'think only of contenting yourself and following your own inclinations, and don't worry at all about me. Nothing matters to me except whatever I see pleases you.'

A few days later Gualtieri sent someone for his son, much as he had done as regards his daughter. After a similar show of having him murdered, he dispatched him to Bologna to be brought up there, like the little girl. What the lady said and showed in her face was no different from before, which stunned Gualtieri. He declared to himself that there wasn't a woman anywhere capable of behaving like that. If he hadn't seen her visceral attachment to the children as long as she had his approval, he would have thought she was glad to see the back of them, but he knew that there was sense and wisdom in her.

His subjects, believing he had had his children killed, strongly condemned him for his cruelty and felt nothing but compassion for the lady. When other ladies sympathized with her for having lost her children in this way, she said only that what pleased her was precisely what pleased the man who had fathered them.

Some years after the little girl's birth, Gualtieri decided it was time to put her capacity for endurance to the ultimate test. He told many of his men that he just could not bear Griselda being his wife any more, and that it was clear to him that marrying her had been a bad juvenile error; he was now going to do all he could to obtain special dispensation from the Pope to take another wife and leave Griselda. Quite a few of his better men took him to task, but he only replied that that was how things had to be. When his lady heard the news, she found herself having to face the idea of going back to her father's house, and perhaps tending the sheep as she had done in the past, with the added prospect of some other lady taking possession of the man to whom she had given all the love she had. She was devastated. But she had borne all the other wrongs that fortune had done her, and she set herself to bear this one with similar fortitude.

A little later Gualtieri arranged for some counterfeit letters to be sent from Rome and gave his subjects to believe that in these the Pope had given him dispensation to marry again and leave Griselda. He had her summoned and addressed her before a crowd of onlookers.

'My lady,' he said, 'thanks to a special concession granted me by the Pope, I can take another wife and let you go. Since my ancestors were from the high nobility and the lords of these lands, whereas yours have always been labourers, I intend that you should no longer be my wife and should go back to Giannucolo's house with the dowry you brought me. After that I shall marry someone I've found who will be appropriate for my station.'

Hearing this, the lady had to make an immense effort, one beyond women's natural capacities, in order to keep back her tears.

'My lord,' she replied, 'I always knew my lowly origins in no way accorded with your own nobility. I was glad to attribute to God and to yourself the position I have enjoyed with you. I have never thought it something I had been given, or treated it as anything more than a loan. Your wish is to recover it. I must make it my wish to let you have it, and I am happy to do so. Here is the ring with which you married me. Take it. You order me to carry away with me the dowry I brought you. That's not something for which you'll need a banker, or for which I'll need a bag or a packhorse. It does not escape me that you took me in naked. If you consider it decent for that body in which I carried the children you fathered to be seen by all and sundry, I shall go away naked. But I beg you that you let me have some payment for the virginity that I brought here and do not take away again by allowing me, over and above my dowry, to have a single shift to wear.'

Gualtieri wanted to weep more than anything else. But his face stayed as hard as ever.

'So you go off with a shift then,' he said.

Everyone round him begged him to make her the gift of a robe, and not let the woman who had been his wife for thirteen years or more be seen leaving his house penniless and utterly humiliated, which was what leaving in just a shift would mean. But their requests came to nothing. So it was in a shift, barefoot and bareheaded, that the lady commended them to God's care, and walked out of her husband's house and back to her father's, amid the weeping and wailing of all who saw her.

Giannucolo had never been able to believe that Gualtieri really wanted his daughter as his wife, expecting every day something like this to happen, and had kept the clothes she was wearing on the morning Gualtieri married her. He brought them out and she put them on. Then she gave herself over to the menial tasks around her father's house that she used to do in the past, valiantly bearing the savage assault that hostile fortune had inflicted on her.

Gualtieri's next step was to pretend to his subjects that he had got himself a daughter of one of the Counts of Panago. In the course of the grandiose preparations for the marriage ceremony, he sent for Griselda to come and see him.

'I'm bringing here as my bride,' he said to her when she arrived, 'this lady I've very recently promised to marry. My intention is to receive her with due honour when she comes here for the first time. You're aware that I don't have ladies in the house who can spruce up the rooms and do all the things required for a festive occasion of this sort. Since you know better than anyone else how this house works, sort out what needs to be done, and also invite a welcome party of ladies you think suitable, and receive them as if you were the lady in charge. Then once the marriage-feast is over, you can go back to your own house.'

His words were so many knives in Griselda's heart. She had never been able to abandon the love she felt for him in the way she had let go of her good fortune.

'My lord, I am willing and ready,' she said.

And so, in a makeshift dress of thick, rough cloth, she went back into the house she had left in just her shift not long before, and began sweeping the chambers and tidying them up, fixing hangings and drapes in the halls, and getting the kitchen ready, doing every single thing with her own hands as if she were nothing but a mere servant-girl. Nor did she stop till she had everything as neat and orderly as the occasion required.

Once she had had invitations sent out on Gualtieri's behalf to all the ladies in the area, the only thing left for her to do was to await the coming festivities. When the day of the wedding-feast arrived, in spite of the poor clothes she had on, she gave every one of the ladies who came a joyful and dignified welcome.

Gualtieri had taken care the children should be properly

brought up in Bologna by his female relative, who had married into the house of the Counts of Panago. The girl was now twelve and the prettiest creature ever, and the boy was six. Gualtieri had written to the relative's husband, asking him to be so good as to bring his daughter and son to Saluzzo, accompanied by an appropriate guard of honour, and to tell everyone that he was bringing the girl to be Gualtieri's wife, with no hint to anyone of who she really was.

This gentleman did as the Marquis asked and set off with the girl, her brother and the guard of honour. After some days, around the time of the morning meal, they arrived in Saluzzo, where they found all the local people and many others from round about waiting for this new bride of Gualtieri. The girl was greeted by the ladies and entered the hall where the tables were laid out. Griselda, dressed just as she was, went towards her happily enough, saying, 'My lady is welcome.'

The other ladies, who had repeatedly but fruitlessly begged Gualtieri either to let Griselda stay in one of the chambers or to lend her one of the robes that were once hers, so that she would not appear before the visitors looking as she did, were now assigned their places at the tables and began to be served. The girl was the object of everybody's attention and the general view was that Gualtieri had made a good exchange. One of those who was most lavish with her praises, both of the girl and of her little brother, was Griselda.

Gualtieri thought he had now had all the proof he could want of the patience of his lady. He could tell that it was not at all affected by events, no matter how bizarre they were, and, given the wisdom he knew was in her, he was sure that dullness of mind was not a factor. He decided it was time to release her from the tortures he judged she must be suffering beneath her calm and steady exterior. He had her come forward and, before everyone who was there, gave her a smile and asked:

'What do you think of our bride?'

'My lord,' replied Griselda, 'I can only think very well of her. If her good sense is equal to her beauty, as I believe it must be, I have no doubt that living with her will make you the most most contented lord in the world. But I beg you with all my heart not to inflict on her the sort of wounds you inflicted on the other one, the one who was your wife before. I can't really believe that she could stand it. She's younger, and what's more she's been brought up in luxury, whereas the other had spent her childhood doing hard physical work.'

Gualtieri could see that she firmly believed that the girl was going to be his wife and yet still said nothing he could disapprove of. He sat her down at his side and then spoke.

'Griselda,' he said, 'it is now time for you to taste the fruit of your steadfast patience and for those who judged me cruel, unjust and inhuman to acknowledge that what I did had a deliberate purpose. I wanted to teach you to be a wife, to teach my critics how to take a wife and to keep one, and to bring about for myself unbroken peace and quiet for as long as my life with you might last. This was something I was very afraid wouldn't happen when I first took a wife. It was to test if it were possible that I inflicted on you the wounds and torments you are all too aware of.

'Since I have never perceived you going against my wishes in anything you have said or done, I judge that I do indeed have from you the contentment I desired. I therefore intend to restore to you in one single moment what I took from you over the years, and to apply the sweetest possible medicine to the wounds I inflicted. So now, with joy in your heart, receive this girl you think is my bride, and her brother too. These are our children that you and many others have long thought I had brutally murdered. And I myself am your husband, who loves you more than anything else. I think I can rightly and honestly boast that no other man alive can be as happy with his wife as I am.'

After this speech he put his arms round her and kissed her. He then raised her to her feet and led her, weeping for joy, over to where their daughter was sitting, astounded by what she was hearing. They tenderly embraced the two children, and then told the girl and many other people there the truth of the situation. The ladies were delighted to get up from the tables and go with Griselda into one of the chambers. Expressing hopes of a better outcome this time, they helped her out of her rough clothing and dressed her in one of her noble robes. Then they led her back into the hall a courtly lady, which even in her rags she had retained the air of being. There followed a moment of marvellous celebration with the children, and everyone showed their joy at the way things had turned out. Then they plunged into fun and merrymaking, which went on for days.

Everyone judged Gualtieri to have shown great wisdom, though they judged the tests inflicted on his lady to have been too severe, indeed intolerable. Griselda they held to have shown more wisdom than anyone.

After some days the Count of Panago returned to Bologna and Gualtieri took Giannucolo away from his work. From then he was treated as a proper father-in-law, and lived very happily and much respected until a ripe old age. After finding a noble husband for his daughter, Gualtieri himself lived a long and happy life with Griselda, and treated her with all possible honour.

What can be said here except that divine spirits descend from heaven even into poor houses and into royal houses come spirits which deserve more to look after pigs than be lords over men? Who else but Griselda could have borne the callous, unprecedented tests Gualtieri subjected her to, not just without tears but with what looked like cheerfulness? Perhaps it would have served him right if the woman he happened to pick had let another man shake her muff when she was driven from home in her shift, and that way got herself a decent dress.

PENGUIN

LITTLE BLACK

CLASSICS

PENGUIN

LITTLE BLACK

CLASSICS

Penguin Little Black Classics Vol. I

01. GIOVANNI BOCCACCIO
Mrs Rosie and the Priest

02. EDGAR ALLAN POE
The Tell-Tale Heart

03. ANTON CHEKHOV
Gooseberries

04. LEO TOLSTOY
How Much Land Does a Man Need?

05. GUSTAVE FLAUBERT
A Simple Heart

06. RYUNOSUKE AKUTAGAWA
The Life of a Stupid Man

07. THOMAS HARDY
The Withered Arm

08. KENKO
A Cup of Sake Beneath the Cherry Trees

09. WILLIAM BLAKE
Tyger Tyger

10. RAINER MARIA RILKE
Letters to a Young Poet

企鹅经典：小黑书　第一辑

01.　贝尔科洛蕾夫人与神父

［意］薄伽丘

02.　泄密的心

［美］爱伦·坡

03.　醋栗

［俄］契诃夫

04.　一个人需要许多土地吗？

［俄］列夫·托尔斯泰

05.　一颗简单的心

［法］福楼拜

06.　傻子的一生

［日］芥川龙之介

07.　萎缩的胳膊

［英］托马斯·哈代

08.　樱花树下的清酒

［日］吉田兼好

09.　虎！虎！

［英］威廉·布莱克

10.　给一个青年诗人的十封信

［奥］里尔克

“当男人们不在家时，
他就去看望他们的女人，
比以往任何一任神父
都要热切……”

PENGUIN

LITTLE BLACK

CLASSICS

* 此中文译本译自意大利语原文

* 书名翻译说明：

意大利语原文中，女主角的名字 Belcolore，音译为贝尔科洛蕾，意为“漂亮的颜色”。在本书的英文译本中，想要保留这层意思，于是选择用 Rosie Hues 来表达。Rosie 本身有“多彩的，玫瑰花般的”意思，而 Hues 是颜色的意思。本蒂韦尼亚 · 德尔 · 马佐的名字 Bentivegna del Mazzo 直译过来的意思是“欢迎疯男人”，英文版译为 Willy Welcome，Willy 是 William（威廉姆）的简称，这个名字本身带着一些疯癫和幽默的味道，姓氏则直接选择了 Welcome（欢迎）这个词，组成一个完整的名字。

贝尔科洛蕾夫人与神父

Mrs Rosie and the Priest

[意] 薄伽丘 著

文铮 王金霄 译

中信出版集团 · 北京

图书在版编目（C I P）数据

企鹅经典·小黑书.第一辑：英、汉 / (日)吉田兼好等著；文东等译. -- 北京：中信出版社，2018.11（2022.7 重印）
书名原文：Penguin Little Black Classics
ISBN 978-7-5086-9400-9

Ⅰ.①企… Ⅱ.①吉… ②文… Ⅲ.①世界文学—作品综合集—英、汉 Ⅳ.①I11

中国版本图书馆 CIP 数据核字 (2018) 第 193780 号

企鹅经典：小黑书　第一辑
贝尔科洛蕾夫人与神父

著　　者：[意]薄伽丘
译　　者：文铮　王金霄
出版发行：中信出版集团股份有限公司
（北京市朝阳区惠新东街甲 4 号富盛大厦 2 座 邮编 100029）
承 印 者：河北鹏润印刷有限公司

开　　本：787mm×1092mm　1/32　　印　　张：41　　字　　数：300 千字
版　　次：2018 年 11 月第 1 版　　印　　次：2022 年 7 月第 13 次印刷
京权图字：01-2018-6477
书　　号：ISBN 978-7-5086-9400-9
定　　价：149.00 元（全 10 册）

服务热线：400-600-8099
投稿邮箱：author@citicpub.com

目录

一个叫安德鲁奇奥的佩鲁贾人在那不勒斯的历险故事[1]

据说，在佩鲁贾有位名叫安德鲁奇奥·迪·皮耶特罗的小伙子，靠贩卖马匹为生。听说那不勒斯的马卖得非常实惠，他便带了五百枚佛罗林金币[2]，与其他商贩一起奔赴那不勒斯了。这是他第一次离开家。周日晚上，将近晚祷的时候，安德鲁奇奥到达了目的地。他从旅馆老板那里打听到，第二天早晨就会有一个马市。马市上

1. 本书中的四个故事均节选自《十日谈》，故事标题为英文译者根据故事内容所起，并非原有标题。本书译文是根据 1980 年艾奥迪（Einaudi）出版社出版的新版《十日谈》翻译的，主编是维托雷·布兰卡（Vittore Branca）。本篇故事原标题为“第二天第五则故事”。（说明：书中脚注均为译者注。）
2. 佛罗林是当时在佛罗伦萨流通的金币。

果真有许多马匹，安德鲁奇奥也看中了好几匹，就上前去跟商贩们讨价还价。为了让对方知道自己能买得起这些马，他就像那些土里土气的乡下人一样，每当有人经过，就把金币从包里掏出来显摆一下。但最终价格并没有谈好，所以他连一匹马都没有买到。

在商量价钱时，他的钱袋子吸引了旁边一位西西里女人的注意。虽然她长得漂亮，但是非常轻浮，为了几个小钱就能把自己随随便便交付给一个男人。趁安德鲁奇奥不注意，她偷偷地靠近了这个小伙子，偷瞄了一眼他的钱袋，心想："要是我有了这些钱，谁还能比得上我呢？"然后，她就悄悄走开了。有一位老妇陪伴在这个女人的身边，她也是西西里人。当看到安德鲁奇奥后，老妇立刻激动地跑过去拥抱这位同乡，完全没有注意到女主人的离开，原来他们早就相识。安德鲁奇奥转脸看到老妇，热情地和她打了招呼，还邀请她有空去自己下榻的旅馆做客。两人没说几句话就各忙各的去了，但是那个女人却躲在一旁，偷听了这两位同乡的对话。

安德鲁奇奥继续逛马市，但始终没有买到马。那女人见他带了那么多钱，又看到他跟自己手下的老妇如此熟络，就仔仔细细地询问老妇关于安德鲁奇奥的情况：

他是谁，从哪里来，到这里做什么，他们是如何认识的，一五一十地统统问了个遍，以便设计陷阱把他的钱弄到手。能把他所有的钱都弄到手自然是好，如果不行，能拿到一部分也是不错的。老妇一五一十地回答了主人的问题，事无巨细，就像是安德鲁奇奥本人在回答似的。老妇之所以如此了解安德鲁奇奥，是因为早年在西西里的时候，她曾在他父亲的手下干活，后来又跟他们一起去了佩鲁贾。她还把安德鲁奇奥住的地方以及他来那不勒斯的原因一并告诉了主人。

那女人掌握了安德鲁奇奥所有的信息，连他家人的名字都一清二楚。如此一来，她就能对安德鲁奇奥行骗，满足自己的贪心了。回家以后，她给老妇安排了很多工作，让她忙得一整天都出不了门，根本没办法找安德鲁奇奥叙旧，她又派手下一名深谙此道的女佣，在晚祷时去安德鲁奇奥住的旅馆找他。

女佣在旅馆门口看到一名男子，便上前打听安德鲁奇奥的情况。碰巧的是，这名男子正是安德鲁奇奥。女佣把他拉到一旁，对他说："先生，有位美丽的姑娘想见您一面，不知您何时方便。"安德鲁奇奥听了以后，上上下下打量了自己一番，觉得自己的确是个美男子，也许

整个那不勒斯再也找不到一位如此英俊的小伙子了。他认为那位姑娘肯定是爱上他了。想到这里，他立刻跟女佣说自己随时都可以过去，便问她那姑娘想什么时候和他交谈。

女佣回答道："先生，无论您何时过去，她都会在家恭候您。"

安德鲁奇奥一听这话，没有和旅馆打声招呼就对女佣说："你在前面带路，我现在就跟你去见她。"

那女人家门前的道路叫"魔窟街"，一看这个名字，就知道这条街上的居民有多么"善良"了。但是安德鲁奇奥并不知道真相，也没有半点疑虑。他相信，在这片美好的土地上，他要找的那位姑娘一定天真而纯良。于是他跟着女佣走进了姑娘家。上楼时，女佣对女主人说："安德鲁奇奥来啦！"安德鲁奇奥也看到了那位在楼梯口等他的姑娘。

她正值青春，身材修长，面容姣好，穿着优雅而得体。看到安德鲁奇奥来了，女人连忙下楼迎接。她张开双臂，紧抱住他的脖子，欲言又止，激动得说不出话来。随后，她潸然泪下，亲吻了他的额头，用近乎沙哑的声音对他说："我的安德鲁奇奥啊！你知道我有多想见到你吗？！"

安德鲁奇奥没有料到会受到如此热烈的欢迎，一时惊讶不已，只好顺着姑娘的话回应道:“天哪！我也很想见到您！”

于是姑娘走到他身旁，牵起他的手，一句话也没有说，就带他走进了自己的闺房。她的房间里洋溢着玫瑰、橘子花和各种香料散发出的芬芳气息，闺床装饰华丽，床架上挂着许多华美的服装，还有很多精致的摆设。安德鲁奇奥还是第一次看到这些东西，这使他更加相信面前这个女人一定是位出身高贵的小姐。

女人请他坐在床边的一个箱子上，开口说道:“安德鲁奇奥，我知道我的热情和激动肯定吓着你了，毕竟你我从未见过面，你也没有听说过我这个人。但听完我接下来给你讲的这件事，你一定会更加惊讶——我可是你的亲姐姐啊！谢天谢地，让我在死前还能亲眼看到我的弟弟！我是多么想见一见我的亲弟弟啊！不然我死也不会瞑目！你好像不知道这回事，那就让我来告诉你吧。我们的父亲皮耶罗曾在巴勒莫住过很长一段时间，我相信你肯定知道这事吧。他和蔼善良，所以周围的人都十分爱戴他，直到今天也都很惦念他，其中最爱他的那个人就是我的母亲。我的母亲出身高贵，但当时正在守

寡。她不顾父兄的威胁恐吓，放弃了自己的尊荣，选择与我们的父亲在一起。后来，我，也就是你面前的这个人，就出生了。再后来，由于突发情况，父亲离开了巴勒莫，去了佩鲁贾。当时我还只是个小女孩，他就抛弃了我们母女二人。我总觉得，他走后就把我们忘得一干二净了！如果他不是我的生身父亲，那我眼看着他如此对待我母亲，一定会怪他冷酷无情！怎奈是他生了我！抛开他辜负了我母亲的一片真情不说，我好歹也是他的女儿啊！更何况我母亲既不是有损他颜面的无知少女，也不是放荡轻浮的风尘女子。她对父亲一片痴心，但却没有看清他的本来面目，就把自己的一切都托付给他了。可是这换回了什么呢？往事说起来容易，但却很难挽回，何况事情已经这样了。他在巴勒莫抛弃我们时，我年龄还小，后来我慢慢长成了现在的模样。我的母亲毕竟是贵族出身，所以把我嫁给了杰尔真蒂[1]那边一位家境富裕的绅士。他深爱着我，也敬重我的母亲，所以搬到了巴勒莫与我们同住。他坚决拥护教皇派[2]，所以和西西里

1. 即今天西西里岛的阿格里琴托城。

2. 12—13 世纪，意大利中部和北部分别支持教皇和神圣罗马帝国，因此分为教皇派与皇帝派两派。双方的纷争在意大利一直持续到 15 世纪。

的查理国王交往甚密。但腓特烈国王察觉了这一切，于是我们只好逃离西西里。那时，我马上就要被封为女骑士了，这种事在西西里岛上还是头一遭。于是我们带着不多的行李——即便‘不多’，其实也不少，只是就那时的家境而言‘不多’罢了，我们离开了那片土地，离开了我们的宫殿，逃到了这里。查理国王感念我们的笃诚，在那不勒斯给了我们田地和房产作为补偿，还一直寄很多钱给我丈夫，也就是你姐夫，这你以后就会看到的。就这样，我在这里住了下来。幸亏天主保佑，而不是拜你所赐，我才又见到了你，我的弟弟。”

说完，她又紧紧地抱住了安德鲁奇奥，亲吻他的额头，眼睛里噙满了泪水。

安德鲁奇奥听完这个故事，觉得一切是那么合情合理，而且这个姑娘在讲故事时也没打一个磕巴。他又想起自己的父亲的确在巴勒莫住过一段时间，那时的父亲和自己现在一样年轻，当然也会贪恋女色。再看看面前姑娘眼含热泪，想想她的拥抱和那些真诚的亲吻，安德鲁奇奥将她说的话信以为真。等她不说话了，安德鲁奇奥开口说道：“您应该料到了我会大吃一惊。我的父亲从未提及过你们母女，或者说他曾经提起过，但我没有听

到，所以我并不认识您，也不知道您的存在。然而能在那不勒斯找到姐姐，的确出乎我的意料，让我十分开心。没有哪位男士不想与您亲近，无论他的地位有多高，更何况是我这个小商贩。但是请您告诉我一件事情，您是怎么知道我在这里的呢？”

那女人答道：“是今天早上一个经常来我家的穷老太太告诉我的，也是她说起了我们的父亲。她告诉我，父亲在巴勒莫和佩鲁贾时，自己一直在他家里做事。我听了这些话，早就想去找你了，可是我一个女人去陌生男子的住处有失体统，所以就把你叫到了这里。”

说完这些，她又询问起了家人的近况，还说出了他们的名字。安德鲁奇奥一一作答，并且越发相信她说的话了——尽管他不该相信。

他们就这样聊了很久。女人让下人端来了白葡萄酒和蜜饯，请安德鲁奇奥享用。安德鲁奇奥喝完酒，看着晚饭时间快到了，便起身告辞。姑娘却无论如何也不答应，还装作生气的样子，抱住他说：“哎呀！你走吧！我算是明白了，你根本就没把我当亲人！我怎么也想象不到，你刚刚见到了从未谋面的姐姐，还在她的家里，却要回旅馆吃饭！对，我的丈夫是没在家，我也很遗憾他

不能陪你用晚餐，但我知道作为一个女人该如何招待你。”

听了这些话，安德鲁奇奥不知该如何回答，只好说：“我是把您当亲人的，就像您对我一样。但是如果我不回去，旅馆的人要等我一晚上才能吃饭，这未免失礼啊。”

女人这时说：“天哪！难道我就不能派家里的用人去趟旅馆，告诉他们不用等你了吗？既然你这么懂得礼数，那就该把旅馆的朋友叫来一起用晚餐。那样吃完饭后，你还可以和他们一起回去。”

安德鲁奇奥说，今晚不想请朋友来，但他非常愿意留下。于是女人假装派人告诉旅馆老板他不回去吃饭的事，又与他聊了很长时间，才吩咐用人上晚餐。晚餐十分丰盛，女人也故意拖延时间。直到夜幕降临，安德鲁奇奥起身告辞时，她仍旧坚持不让他走，说是因为在那不勒斯晚上不能出门随便走动，尤其是一个外地人。她还说，刚刚让人跟旅馆说他不回去吃饭时，也交代过他不回去过夜了。安德鲁奇奥觉得这些话有道理，而且他很想和姑娘在一起，所以就又被她骗了。他们接着聊了好一阵——这当然也是女人故意而为的。夜深了，她让安德鲁奇奥到自己的卧室睡下，又留下了一个侍童伺候，看他不再需要什么了，便带着侍女们去了另一个房间。

天气十分炎热，安德鲁奇奥看房间里只剩他一个人了，就把裤子、袜子和内衣全部脱掉，放在了床头。过了一会儿，他想去方便，就问侍童厕所在哪里。侍童指着一扇门说：“进去吧，这里就是。”安德鲁奇奥毫无戒备地走进了那扇门，不料踏到了一块架空的木板上，连人带板一起摔了下去。幸亏天主保佑，虽然从很高的地方摔下，但他并没有受伤。只是掉下去的地方满是污秽，所以他浑身散发着恶臭。为了让你们明白我刚刚讲的内容，也为了方便你们理解接下来发生的事，我得在这里啰唆几句。他掉下去的那个地方其实在一个小巷子里，就像我们经常可以看到的那样：人们在对着的两个窗户间搭上两根细细的木棍，然后在木棍上架一块木板，人就坐在木板上方便。安德鲁奇奥就是从这样一块木板上掉下去的。

安德鲁奇奥摔得很疼。他发现自己掉到了小巷子里，就连忙喊侍童。然而侍童一听到他掉下去的声响，就跑到女人那里报信去了。那女人赶紧去他房间，看他的衣服在不在。找到衣服后，从里面翻出了安德鲁奇奥的钱。原来他不放心把钱放到别处，都是随身带着。这位“巴勒莫的贵妇”，这位“佩鲁贾小伙子的姐姐”，拿到钱之

后，就再也不管安德鲁奇奥的安危，关上了他方才走出去的那扇门。

安德鲁奇奥看侍童没有回答他，就更大声地喊叫，但已然没有用了。这时他才感觉到有些不对，可是为时已晚。安德鲁奇奥翻过一道矮墙，到了大街上。他认识姑娘的家门，便过去不停地敲打，不停地叫喊，但还是没人理睬他。这时他才知道自己被骗了，哭着说："哎呀！才这么一小会儿，我就丢了五百个金币和一个姐姐啊！"

哭了一阵子后，他又开始敲门喊人。邻居们受不了他的闹腾，纷纷起身。那家的一个女佣装作被吵醒的样子，朝窗外怒吼："谁在下面敲门呢？"

"喂！"安德鲁奇奥说，"你不认识我了？我是安德鲁奇奥啊，菲奥尔达莉索夫人的弟弟！"

女佣回答他说："你这个人！如果你喝多了，就先睡一觉，明早再过来吧！我既不认识安德鲁奇奥，也听不懂你说的话。请你走吧，让我们好生休息，拜托了！"

"怎么会？"安德鲁奇奥说，"难道你不知道我说的是什么吗？你绝对知道！就算你们西西里人对待亲戚都是转脸就忘，但至少让我把留在你们家的衣服拿走吧！我拿了衣服会立刻走人！"

女佣快要笑出声来了，说:“我看你这人是在梦游吧！”边说边缩回身子，关上了窗子。

安德鲁奇奥这才恍然大悟，原来自己被骗了，他气得快要发疯。但现在光靠嘴已经拿不回想要的东西了，于是他拿起一块大石头使劲砸门。他的动静更大了，吵醒了更多的邻居，惹得他们十分反感。邻居们相信他就是个骗子，编这些谎话来骚扰那位善良的夫人。于是他们都到窗边责骂安德鲁奇奥，就像是满街的狗对着一只新来的狗狂吠一样。“你这个时候来人家姑娘家，说这些不三不四的话，实在无礼！”“天哪！你走吧，好孩子，让我们睡觉吧，求你了！”“你要是真有事找她，就明天再来吧，今晚就别烦我们了！”

那位“好姑娘”的家里还住着一个恶棍。不过安德鲁奇奥在她家时既没有看到他，也没有听到他说话。听到邻居们这么说，恶棍放心了，于是走到窗前，粗声粗气地吼道:“是谁在下面？”

安德鲁奇奥听到这吓人的声音，抬起头来，隐隐约约地瞧见这个满脸黑胡子的人，看样子很厉害。只见他伸着懒腰，打着呵欠，像刚从床上爬起来似的。安德鲁奇奥见状，不免有些害怕地回答道:“我是这家女主人的

弟弟。”

然而那人没等他说完，就打断了他，语气比之前还要凶：“我不知道我为什么还站在这儿，而不是下去给你一通乱棍，把你打到不能动弹为止。你这个醉鬼，你这个烦人的蠢驴，今天晚上因为你谁都睡不成觉了！”说罢便缩回身子，锁上了窗户。

一些邻居知道这个人的脾气，就低声劝安德鲁奇奥说：“求你了，好孩子，走吧！你不想今晚被他打死吧！走吧，这是为你好。”

安德鲁奇奥害怕那个恶棍，又被邻居们这么一劝，觉得他们也是好心，就离开了。一想到自己再也拿不回那些钱，他非常难过。安德鲁奇奥不知道去哪里，只好沿着女佣带他来时走过的路回旅馆。但是他身上很臭，想去海里洗一洗，就在路口往左拐，走进了一条叫作“卡塔拉纳”的街。他顺着坡往上走，突然看见两个提着灯笼的人向自己走来。安德鲁奇奥担心对方是巡警，也害怕又遇到坏人，于是看旁边有个小破屋，就悄悄地躲了进去。然而那两个人像是提前商量好了似的，径直走进了这间破屋子。其中一个人把背在肩上的铁家伙放了下来，和另一个人一起一一查看。

突然，其中一个人说：“怎么回事？我闻见了一股臭味，之前好像从来没在这儿闻见过。”他说完便举起灯笼，看到了可怜的安德鲁奇奥。这人吓了一跳，问道：“谁在那里？”

安德鲁奇奥没有出声，于是那两个人拿着灯笼走近了他，问他一身脏臭的在这里干什么。安德鲁奇奥就把事情的来龙去脉一五一十地告诉了他们。他们想了一下这件事发生的地方，自言自语地说：“那是布塔福科家，就是那个黑社会的小头目。”

其中一个人对安德鲁奇奥说：“可怜的家伙，虽然你把钱丢了，但你还算是万幸，因为你幸亏摔了下来，没再进那座房子。要是你没有摔下去，他们肯定等你一睡着就把你杀了，那样你连钱带命就都丢了。你现在哭有什么用呢？想拿回一分钱，比从天上摘星星还要难呢。而且，他们要是知道你把这件事说了出去，可能还会来杀你。”

他说完后，两个人商量了一会儿，又对安德鲁奇奥说：“你看，我们很同情你。现在我们正要去做点事情，如果你加入我们，那我们保证你能赚到比你丢掉的那五百个金币更多的钱。”

正走投无路的安德鲁奇奥立刻答应了。

原来那天是那不勒斯大主教菲利波·米努托洛神父下葬的日子。他穿的华服上有许多价值连城的饰品，手上还戴着一枚红宝石戒指。光是那块红宝石就值五百多佛罗林，而那两个人想偷的也正是它。就这样，他们把计划告诉了安德鲁奇奥。

安德鲁奇奥的欲望战胜了理智，便和他们一起上路了。在去往主教堂的路上，安德鲁奇奥仍然一身臭气，于是他们中的一人说道：“我们不能找个地方让他稍微洗洗吗？免得他这么臭。”

另一个人回答说：“对，这附近有一口井，井辘轳上一直挂着个大木桶。我们赶紧去那里让他洗一洗吧。”

到了井边，他们发现绳子还在，但是木桶被人拿走了。于是那两人想着用绳子拴住安德鲁奇奥，让他下井清洗一下，洗好了晃绳子，他们再把他拉上来。就这样，安德鲁奇奥下井了。

他刚下去，就来了几个巡警。因为天气炎热，又刚刚追捕了一个犯人，所以他们口渴难耐，就来井边找水喝。那两个人一看到巡警来了，撒腿就跑，所以巡警并没有看到他们。

安德鲁奇奥在井底洗好后晃了绳子。看到绳子晃了，那两个口渴的巡警以为桶里的水满了，就把手里的木盾、武器和披风放在地上，往上拉绳子。安德鲁奇奥看到井沿后，就抓着井沿跳了上来。巡警看到从井里跳出来了一个人，吓得魂飞魄散，立刻松开了绳子，跑得要多快有多快。安德鲁奇奥自己也大吃了一惊，要不是抓住了井沿，他就可能摔到井底，也就可能受伤乃至丢了性命。他又看到了井边的武器，便更加疑惑了，因为他记得那两个同伴并没有带什么武器。

他心存疑虑，不知道发生了什么事情。于是什么都没碰，离开了那个地方，但又不知道去哪里。就这样走着走着，他突然碰见了之前的两个同伴。原来，他们想回去把安德鲁奇奥拉上来。看到安德鲁奇奥后，同伴们也十分惊讶，连忙问是谁把他拉上来的。安德鲁奇奥说自己也不知道，只把从井里上来的经过告诉了他们。两人相视一笑，明白了怎么回事，向安德鲁奇奥解释了他们为什么逃走，又是谁拉他上来的。这时夜已过半，所以大家就没有再多说什么，直接去主教堂了。他们很顺利地进了教堂，来到了大主教的棺材旁。这口棺材很大，而且是用大理石做的。他们用随身带的铁棍撬起了沉重的

棺材盖，然后找东西撑住，留出来够一个人出入的空隙。

做好后，他们其中一人说：“谁进去？”

另一个人回答：“我不去。”

“我也不去，”那个人说，“安德鲁奇奥，你去。”

“我不会去的。”安德鲁奇奥说。

听了这话，那两人对安德鲁奇奥说：“你为什么不去？苍天在上，要是你不进去，我们就用这根铁棍打你的头，直到打死你为止。”

安德鲁奇奥很害怕，只好进去。他一边往里爬一边想：“他们让我进来，无非是想骗我。等到我把东西给了他们，要往外爬时，他们就会自顾自地跑了，而我什么也得不到。”因此他决定先把自己那份弄到手。安德鲁奇奥想起他们之前说的话，就把那枚昂贵的戒指从大主教手上摘了下来，戴在了自己手上。然后他把主教的权杖、僧帽、手套给了那两个人，跟他们说里面什么也没有了。的确，当时的主教身上只剩一件衬衣了。那两个人确定里面有一枚戒指，就让安德鲁奇奥再好好找找。安德鲁奇奥假装努力地找，一直跟他们说没有找到，让他们在外面等。谁知那两个人比安德鲁奇奥还要狡猾，不停地说让他再找找，却趁机拿掉了撑着棺盖的东西，逃了出

去，把安德鲁奇奥一个人留在了棺材里。我们应该可以想象出安德鲁奇奥当时的心情吧。

他用头和肩膀顶棺盖，尝试了许多次，但始终没有顶开。一阵绝望袭来，安德鲁奇奥昏倒在了大主教的尸体上。要是有人看见这一幕，一定分不清到底哪个是死人，也分不清谁是大主教，谁是安德鲁奇奥。醒来后，安德鲁奇奥不禁号啕大哭。他预料到，自己只会有两种结局：如果没有人来打开棺材，那他只能在这里面，在一堆蛆虫中饿死，或者被尸体腐烂的臭味熏死；如果有人来开棺，那么他就会被当作盗墓贼绞死。

就在悲痛万分地思考这些事情时，安德鲁奇奥突然听到有很多人边说话边走进了教堂。他认为这些人来这里，也要干那两个人干过的勾当。于是他更害怕了。但是等他们打开了棺盖，撑好之后，也遇到了派谁进去的问题。他们谁都不想进去，吵了很长时间以后，一位神父说：“你们有什么好怕的？觉得他能吃了你们？死人是不会吃人的。来，我进去。”说罢，神父把胸脯抵在棺材沿上，脸向外，将腿伸了进去。安德鲁奇奥一看到他，就马上站了起来，抓住他的一条腿，装作要把他拉下来的样子。神父感到有东西在拽自己，吓得大叫起来，立

刻爬出棺材逃走了。其他人看到这番情形也都吓坏了，没把棺材盖合上就撒腿跑了，好像身后有千万个魔鬼在追赶他们一样。

安德鲁奇奥看到这些后喜出望外，赶紧爬了出来，沿着来时的路走出了教堂。天快亮了，安德鲁奇奥戴着那枚历经千难万险才得到的戒指，走到了海边，然后回到了旅馆。旅馆的店主和他的朋友们为他担心了整整一宿。安德鲁奇奥把这一夜发生的事情告诉他们后，店主建议他赶紧离开那不勒斯。于是他立刻出发，回佩鲁贾去了。安德鲁奇奥原本打算拿了五百枚金币买马，结果马没买成，却换来了一枚戒指。

里卡尔多·钦齐卡失去了他的妻子[1]

从前，在比萨有一位法官大人，名叫里卡尔多·迪·钦齐卡，虽然体力衰弱，但却十分聪明。法官很富有，想找一位年轻美丽的妻子。他觉得，对待妻子只需要拿出做学问的精力就可以了。他找得很慢，心想，如果帮自己拿主意也像帮别人拿主意一样简单，那他早就选好妻子了。最后，他如愿以偿地找到了一位年轻貌美的妻子——洛托·瓜兰迪先生把自己的女儿许配给了他。这位姑娘叫巴尔托洛梅娅，是比萨最美丽可人的姑娘之一。在比萨，毕竟没有几个人长得比吃虫子的蜥蜴更好看。法官举行了盛大的庆典迎娶姑娘，婚礼豪华而又隆重。

1. 原标题为“第二天第十则故事”。

新婚之夜，为了遵守惯例，他勉强与妻子做了一次爱，但是很快就招架不住了。第二天早上，本就瘦弱的他已然筋疲力尽，只能靠干白葡萄酒、滋补蜜饯和其他补品来恢复体力。

现在这位法官大人比之前更清楚自己的能力了，于是开始教妻子读一本历书。这本历书好像是在拉文纳出版印制的，很受孩子们的喜爱。[1]根据这本历书上的标注，每一天都会纪念一位圣人，甚至在一天之内要纪念好几位圣人。法官用了很多理由向妻子解释说，为了表示崇敬之心，男女在这些日子里都要禁欲，不能行房事。除了历书上规定的节日以外，他还增加了斋戒日、四季小斋、圣徒斋戒日，还有纪念千余位圣人的斋戒日，又添上了礼拜五、礼拜六和献给天主的礼拜日。除此之外，禁欲的日子还有整个四旬斋期间。里卡尔多还规定了上百个方位，一旦月亮移动到这些位置，男女就不可行房。此外，在其他一些特殊情况下，夫妻也要禁欲。他觉得，对待同床的女人，就像应对法律案件，没什么不同。这么一来，他的太太要吃不少苦头。里卡尔多一个月只碰

1. 据说，一年中有多少天，在拉文纳城中就有多少座教堂。每天都是纪念圣人的节日，都要休假，所以孩子们很喜欢这本历书。

她一次，而且把她盯得死死的，以防有人像自己教她什么是节假日那样教她什么是工作日。

夏天到了，天气炎热，里卡尔多大人想带妻子一起去蒙特内罗附近的庄园里住几天，避暑消遣。这一天，里卡尔多为了让太太开心，便带她去海上钓鱼。他和渔夫坐在一只船上，妻子和侍女们坐在另一只船上。大家一时兴起，一直驶向了深海，驶出了好几海里还未曾察觉。大家要么专心致志地钓鱼，要么聚精会神地观看。就在这时，突然驶来一艘大船，那是当时远近闻名的海盗帕伽尼诺的船。看到两只小船，帕伽尼诺径直地驶了过去。小船只能拼命地逃，但是海盗还是追上了法官太太坐的船。帕伽尼诺看到船上美丽的夫人，就想也不想地把她掳走了。这时的里卡尔多已经上岸，只能眼睁睁地看着海盗把他夫人带上船，消失在茫茫大海上。法官本就心胸狭窄，连空气都要嫉妒，现在看到这一幕有多恼火，就不必我多言了吧。他到比萨控诉海盗的恶行，又去了其他地方，但最终也没能得知是谁抢走了妻子，又把她带去了哪里。

帕伽尼诺看巴尔托洛梅娅如此美丽，不禁心动。再加上他本就没有妻室，所以就想和她永远生活在一起。

巴尔托洛梅娅大哭不止，帕伽尼诺就温柔地安慰她。夜幕降临，他解开了她的腰带。那本历书刚好从腰带上掉了下来，与此同时，每一个节日和休假日都从她的脑海中消失了。帕伽尼诺觉得实际行动比话语有效，就一直用行动安慰她。就这样，还没到摩纳哥，巴尔托洛梅娅就把法官和他的规定忘得一干二净，和帕伽尼诺过上了天下最快活的日子。帕伽尼诺把巴尔托洛梅娅带到摩纳哥后，不仅日夜宽慰她，还像对待妻子一样善待她。

过了一段时间，里卡尔多大人打听到了太太的下落，便迫不及待地想去找她。他觉得没有人知道该怎么做，于是亲自去找夫人，并且决定无论花多少钱都要赎回她。他乘船去了摩纳哥，见到了巴尔托洛梅娅。巴尔托洛梅娅也看到了里卡尔多，当晚就告诉了帕伽尼诺这件事，并且向他表明了自己的想法。第二天早上，里卡尔多看到帕伽尼诺后就过去和他套近乎。没过多长时间，两人就成了亲密的好友。其实帕伽尼诺认识他，并且知道他想做什么，只是没有表现出来。里卡尔多见时机成熟，就委婉地向帕伽尼诺解释了自己来这里的缘由，接着又央求帕伽尼诺，只要把妻子还给他，不管多少赎金他都会照付。

帕伽尼诺和善地回答道："法官阁下，我很欢迎您的到来，所以我向您简单地解释一下，我家的确有位年轻的姑娘，但我并不知道她是您的太太还是其他人的太太。我不晓得您是谁，对她也不太了解，因为她住在我家没多长时间。我看您是位正直的绅士，就带您去见见她吧。如果真如您所说，那她肯定认识您。如果她说的和您一致，并且想和您回去，看在您如此友善的分儿上，无论您给我多少赎金我都会放她走；如果她说的和您不同，那您就是存心来我这里抢她了。我是个年轻的男子，和其他人一样，也会保护自己的女人，尤其是她，因为我从未见过如此可爱的姑娘。"

里卡尔多说："她绝对是我的妻子，你只要带我去见她就知道了。她一见我，就会立刻勾住我的脖子。你提的意见很好，我非常同意。"

"那么，"帕伽尼诺说，"我们走吧。"

于是两人来到了帕伽尼诺家，在客厅就座。这时，帕伽尼诺派人叫巴尔托洛梅娅过来。她穿戴整齐，从房里走出，来到了里卡尔多和帕伽尼诺所在的客厅。但她见了里卡尔多后，就像见了帕伽尼诺带回家的一位陌生客人似的，只是打了声招呼，并没有多余的举动。法官

原想着巴尔托洛梅娅见了自己会非常开心，所以看到这一幕后十分惊讶，自言自语道：“可能是我失去她后，太过悲伤痛苦，所以面容憔悴，以至于她认不出我了。”

于是他说：“夫人，带你去钓鱼让我付出了多么昂贵的代价啊！我从来没有像失去你之后这样痛苦过，而你却疏远我，好像不认识我了。你没看见吗？我是你的里卡尔多啊！我来这里是要带你回去，不管这家的主人要什么我都会给他。他也很慷慨，无论我付多少赎金都会把你还给我。”

夫人转向他，面带微笑地说：“先生，您是在对我说话吗？您仔细看看，不要把我认成别人了，因为我不记得曾经见过您。”

里卡尔多说：“瞧你说的什么话，你好好看看我，你要是愿意仔细回想一下的话，就会知道我是你的丈夫里卡尔多·迪·钦齐卡。”

夫人说：“先生，请您原谅我，按您说的，我仔细地看了看您，这好像不大礼貌，但不用仔细看，我也知道自己从未见过您。”

里卡尔多又想，她是因为害怕帕伽尼诺，才不敢在他面前承认认识自己。所以过了一会儿，他恳求帕伽尼

诺，让他们两人单独在一个房间里谈一谈。帕伽尼诺说可以，前提是里卡尔多不能强行亲吻她。帕伽尼诺让巴尔托洛梅娅跟着里卡尔多去里屋，听听他想说什么，想怎么回答就怎么回答。

于是他们二人单独去了一间屋子里。一坐下来，里卡尔多就说："啊！我的心肝，我的魂，我活下去的希望啊！现在你不认识爱你胜过爱自己的里卡尔多了吗？怎么能这样呢？我的样子变了那么多吗？啊，你美丽的眼睛啊，看看我吧，哪怕只看一小会儿也行啊。"

巴尔托洛梅娅开始大笑，没有让他再说下去："您明明知道我没有失忆！我并非不知道您是我的丈夫里卡尔多·迪·钦齐卡大人，但是当我和您在一起时，您没有真正地理解过我。如果您像自己以为的那般聪明，那您就应该明白，我年轻活泼，朝气蓬勃，所以和其他少妇一样，除了吃穿外，还会想要别的东西，尽管我害羞说不出口。而您是怎么做的，您自己清楚。如果比起妻子，您更喜欢研究法律的话，那您就不应该娶亲。但我觉得您根本就不是什么法官，只是那些节日和斋戒日的鼓吹者罢了。我跟您说，如果您也让给您种地的农民们过您规定的那些节日，让他们也像您耕种我这块田地一样种

田的话，那您一粒粮食也收获不到。上帝看我年轻，怜悯我，让我遇到了他。我和他就睡在这间房里。在这里，没有人知道节日是什么。我指的节日就是您平时过的那些纪念日。您对上帝的虔诚超越了您对女人的爱。在这扇门里，我们没有礼拜五和礼拜六，没有斋戒日，没有四季小斋，也没有那漫长的四旬斋。相反，我们从早到晚都在‘劳作’，把毯子都扯破了。今天一大早，我还爬到他身上了呢。我愿意和他在一起，趁着年轻好好‘劳作’。那些节日、朝觐和斋戒就留给我的晚年吧。我为您祝福，但请您赶紧离开吧，能多快离开就多快离开。没有我在身旁，您想过多少节日就过多少节日吧。”

里卡尔多听到这些话，感到一阵难以忍受的痛苦，看她停了下来，才说：“啊，我的魂啊！你说的这叫什么话？你现在就不能考虑一下你家人的声望和你的名誉吗？你情愿道德败坏地在这里做他的姘妇，也不想回比萨做我的太太吗？这个男人，当他对你厌烦时，会对你恶语相加，把你赶走的。而我会永远爱你，哪怕我死了，你也会是我家的女主人。为了这点荒淫的肉欲，你就要抛弃你我的名誉，抛弃爱你胜过爱自己生命的我吗？啊，我的亲爱的，我的希望啊！不要再这么说了，跟我回去

吧。我知道你的欲望了，从今往后我会努力的。我的美人儿，你就改变主意，跟我走吧！我从来没有像你离开我之后那么伤心。”

巴尔托洛梅娅回答他说:“我的名誉只能把握在我自己手里，容不得他人说三道四。我再也不会像从前那般温柔恭顺了。如果能回到我父母把我嫁给你的那天，该有多好啊！当时他们没有顾及过我的名誉，现在我也不会考虑他们的声望。如果我现在是个罪恶的‘臼’，那您就是个没用的‘捣槌’。我已经不爱您了。我还要告诉您，在这里，我觉得自己是帕伽尼诺的妻子，而在比萨，我却觉得是您的姘妇。我要想着月亮的方位，研究几何学的规则，才能将我们的‘星体’结合在一起。但在这里，帕伽尼诺每晚都搂我入怀，紧紧抱着我，轻轻地咬我。他是怎么对待我的，就请天主替我告诉您吧。您还说您会努力，可您会努力做什么呢？您能在做完三次后，还能随时坚挺得像个鱼竿似的吗？我知道，在我不在您身边的这些日子里，您已经荣升为骑士了。所以您还是走吧，还是努力地活下去吧。我看您体弱多病，觉得您应该活得很累吧。我再跟您多说一句，即便那人离开了我——不过我觉得不会的，只要我想和他在一起的

话——我也永远不会回到您的身边，因为不管我怎么挤，也不能从您身上挤出一滴‘汁液’。在您那里，我承受了惨痛的损失，现在我要在另一个地方收获利润。我再向您重申一遍，这里没有节日，也没有斋戒日，所以我想留在这里。您赶紧走吧，不然我就叫了，说您要强暴我。”

里卡尔多看情况不妙，只好痛苦万分地走出了那间屋子。直到那时他才明白自己有多无能，而娶一个年轻的妻子又是一件多么荒唐的事情。他又和帕伽尼诺说了很多话，但却无济于事。最后，他什么事也没做成，只能离开妻子，回比萨去了。由于太过悲痛，他已经神智不清，在比萨街头到处游走。无论谁向他打招呼，或者询问事情，他都只会回答说：“坏人是不过节的。”不久之后，他就一命呜呼了。

帕伽尼诺知道巴尔托洛梅娅对自己的爱，就娶了她，让她做了自己的合法妻子。他们从不理会节日和斋戒日，也不过四旬斋，只要腿还能动，就每夜“劳作”。

贝尔科洛蕾夫人与神父[1]

正如你们中的一些人知道，或是曾经听说过的那样：在瓦尔隆戈，也就是离这儿不远的村子里，有一个身强体壮的教士，在服务女人时很能干。尽管学识浅薄，他每逢礼拜日都会在村里的榆树下，说很多好听的善言善语，让村民们开心。当男人们不在家时，他就去看望他们的女人，比以往任何一任神父都要热切，给她们带些宗教节日上的礼品，有时还把圣水和蜡烛头带到家里为她们祝祷。人们还从未见过像他这样的教士呢。

事情是这样的。在之前爱慕过的众多农妇中，他最喜欢的那人名叫贝尔科洛蕾，是农民本蒂韦尼亚·德

1. 原标题为“第八天第二则故事”。

尔·马佐的妻子。贝尔科洛蕾神采奕奕，的确是个讨人喜爱的农妇。她皮肤黝黑，健壮有力，推起磨来比其他女人更有劲。她还会敲铃鼓，唱《水流深谷》，跳力达舞和巴隆基奥舞，兴起时还会从手边拿起一块精致的小手绢舞动，十分俊俏美丽。教士大人喜欢这一切喜欢得不得了，对她着了迷。为了看她，教士整日在村子里逛来逛去。周日早晨，如果见她来了教堂，他就会在唱《慈悲经》和《三圣颂》时特别卖力，来表现自己优秀的歌唱才能，尽管他的声音像驴叫一样难听；如果没有看到她，他就唱得有气无力。尽管知道教士歌声的变化，本蒂韦尼亚·德尔·马佐却丝毫没有察觉到教士对妻子的喜爱，就连他身旁的贝尔科洛蕾也没有意识到这回事。为了和贝尔科洛蕾更亲近些，教士时不时地送她礼物：有时是一把新鲜的大蒜，那是他亲手在菜园里种出来的，也是这片教区中长得最好的蒜；有时是一小筐豆子；有时是一小束五月葱或是一小把斯卡洛尼葱。一有时机，他就用眼神和她打情骂俏。但贝尔科洛蕾对教士很冷漠，举止十分端庄，每次都假装没有看到他，所以教士始终不能如愿以偿。

有一天的正午时分，教士在教区里东走西逛，突然

看到本蒂韦尼亚·德尔·马佐赶着一驾驴车迎面而来，车上载满了东西。于是教士过去和他打招呼，问他要去哪里。

本蒂韦尼亚回答他说：“尊敬的神父，我要去城里办点事情，把这些东西送给博纳科里·达·吉内斯特雷托大人。不知道为什么，一位刑事法官让手下的检察官发了张诉状，里面竟然提到了我。这件事刻不容缓，我想请吉内斯特雷托大人帮帮忙。”

教士高兴地说：“孩子，好好做！带上我的祝福出发吧，快去快回。如果碰到拉普乔或者纳尔迪诺，别忘了跟他们说把我打谷棒上的皮带还给我。”

本蒂韦尼亚答应了他，就朝着佛罗伦萨的方向走了。教士想，是时候去找贝尔科洛蕾碰碰运气了，于是大步向她家走去。他边进门边说：“求天主为这家人赐福！家里有人吗？”

贝尔科洛蕾当时在阁楼里，听到教士的声音，答道：“神父，欢迎您！这么大热的天，您来这里做什么呢？”

教士回答说：“天主赐福于我，我看到你丈夫去城里了，所以过来和你待一会儿。”

贝尔科洛蕾从阁楼下来，坐下收拾丈夫刚打下来的卷心菜种子。教士开口说道：“你看，贝尔科洛蕾，你总

是这个样子，是想急死我吗？”

贝尔科洛蕾笑了，说：“我对您做什么了呀？”

教士说：“你什么都没做，可是你不让我做我想做的事。那件事也是天主让我做的。”

贝尔科洛蕾说：“啊！您清醒一点，教士还做这种事吗？”

教士答道：“我们也做啊，为什么不做呢？我还告诉你，我们的功夫比别的男人还要好。你知道为什么吗？因为我们很少干这事，所以干起来更有劲。说实话，只要安安静静地让我施展，你是会占便宜的。”

贝尔科洛蕾说：“我能占什么便宜呢？你们这些比小气鬼还小气的人！”

于是教士说道：“我不知道你想要什么，所以你自己说吧。你是想要双鞋呢，还是想要个项圈？或者是一块上好的羊毛料子？你想要什么都可以。”

贝尔科洛蕾回答道：“神父，您说得倒好听！这些东西我都有。但是，如果您真的喜欢我，就帮我个忙吧！帮了我的忙，您想做什么，我就让您做什么。”

于是教士说：“你想让我做什么就直说吧，我很愿意帮你。”

贝尔科洛蕾说："周六，我要去趟佛罗伦萨，把我织好的羊毛交给别人，还要修一下我的纺车。如果您借我五里拉，我就能从放高利贷的人手里赎回我那件紫黑色的裙子，还有我那条当嫁妆带过来的腰带。要是没有裙子和腰带，我什么好地方都去不了，也不能去教堂了。我知道，您是有这个钱的。您要是借给我钱，让我做什么我都会做的。"

教士回答说："求天主祝福我！我今天没有带那么多钱，但你相信我，周六之前我会给你的。"

"是吗！"贝尔科洛蕾说，"你们个个都是耍嘴皮子的，却从不履行诺言。您还想用对待毕廖扎的方式对待我，让我所有的期待都落空，然后灰溜溜地离开吗？毕廖扎因为这件事，还沦落成了妓女。我对天发誓，我是不会让您得逞的。所以，如果没有钱，那您就走吧。"

"啊！"教士说，"别让我现在回家拿钱了。你看，我难得那么走运，赶上你家里没人的好时候。要是我回家一趟，等我再回来时，可能就会有人打扰我们了。现在这么好的机会，我不知道要等到什么时候才能再碰上一回。"

贝尔科洛蕾说："说得好听。如果您想回去拿钱，那

就回去，不然您就忍着吧。”

教士看这样子，觉得如果不押给她点东西，她就不会让他做自己想做的事情，于是说道：“你看，你不相信我会给你钱，那我把这件深蓝色的披风押在你这里。这回你相信我了吧。”

贝尔科洛蕾抬头看了一眼说：“哦，这件披风啊。一件披风能值多少钱呢？”

教士说：“值多少钱？我要让你知道，这可是第戎[1]料子，甚至是‘第戎中的第戎料子’，还有人说它是‘特等第戎料子’呢。我从旧货商洛托那里花了整整七里拉才把它买下来，买回家还不到十五天。你知道，洛托最懂这种料子了，他还说我占了五索尔多[2]的便宜呢。”

“哦，这样吗？”贝尔科洛蕾说，“天主保佑，我之前真不敢相信一件披风居然值这么些钱。但是你得先把它给我才行。”

教士大人感到弓已上弦，实在忍不住了，于是急忙把披风脱下来给了她。贝尔科洛蕾把它放好后，对教士说：“大人，请您来棚屋里，这儿不会有人来的。”于是

---

1. 第戎是一座法国城市，盛产羊毛制品。

2. 索尔多是意大利当时的流通货币之一，一里拉等于二十索尔多。

他们去了棚屋。

在屋里，教士给她世上最甜蜜的吻，让她快活得飘飘欲仙。他从贝尔科洛蕾家离开时，像刚为别人主持完婚礼似的，只穿了教士袍，没有穿披风。

回到教堂后，教士想，就算收上整整一年的蜡烛头，连五里拉的一半都赚不到。于是他觉得自己做了件错事，后悔把披风留给了她，开始琢磨该怎么不费分文地把披风要回来。教士这人本来就挺狡猾，所以不一会儿就想出了要回披风的办法。正好第二天是个节日，教士就让邻居家的孩子去贝尔科洛蕾家，问她愿不愿意把石臼借给他，因为宾古焦·达尔·波焦和努托·布列蒂要和他一起用午餐，所以他想用石臼捣些酱汁。于是贝尔科洛蕾把石臼给了那孩子。

到了用午餐的时候，教士偷看到贝尔科洛蕾和丈夫本蒂韦尼亚·德尔·马佐在一起吃饭，便叫来手下的人，对他说："你把这个石臼还给贝尔科洛蕾，然后跟她说'大人非常感谢您，请您把那孩子上午押在您这里的披风还给大人。'"那人来到贝尔科洛蕾家，看到她正和丈夫一起吃饭，就放下了石臼，把教士交代的话说了一遍。

那贝尔科洛蕾听完正想回嘴，不料本蒂韦尼亚脸色阴沉地看着她说：“你敢拿神父大人的东西？我向基督发誓，我真想狠狠地揍你一拳。你这个混账娘们儿，赶紧把东西还回去！听着，无论神父大人要什么东西，哪怕是咱们家的驴，你也不能对他说一个‘不’字。”

贝尔科洛蕾嘟哝着站了起来，从床下的箱子里拿出披风，给了那个人，并且对他说：“你替我告诉大人：‘贝尔科洛蕾向天主祈祷，希望您再也不要在她的“臼”里捣“酱汁”了。在这件事上，您已经失去了她的信任。’”

那人带着披风回去了，并且向教士转告了贝尔科洛蕾的话。教士听了后笑着说：“下次你见到她，就跟她说，她不借给我‘臼’，我还不借给她‘捣槌’了呢。一报还一报吧！”

本蒂韦尼亚听了这些话，还以为神父大人在责怪自己，就没往那件事上想，但贝尔科洛蕾对教士却是爱搭不理。直到收获葡萄的季节[1]，教士恐吓她，如果再不理他，她会被魔王撒旦吃掉。贝尔科洛蕾很害怕，就在酿

1. 即夏季。

葡萄酒和炒栗子的季节[1]里，表面上与他和好了。后来，他们又一起寻欢作乐了很多次。为了补偿那五里拉，教士给她的铃鼓换了张新皮，又系了一个铃铛。贝尔科洛蕾这才开心了。

1. 即秋季。

耐心的格利赛尔达[1]

很久以前，桑卢佐有一个侯爵世家。家中的主人很年轻，名叫瓜尔蒂耶里，尚未娶亲。而且他每天只管打鸟狩猎，根本没有娶妻生子的念头。尽管人们都十分尊敬侯爵，觉得他机智过人，但他手下的人却颇有微词。他们几次三番求他成家，不然侯爵将后继无人，他们也就没有了主公。此外，他们还给侯爵找了许多与他门当户对的姑娘，希望他能喜欢。

侯爵对下属们说："朋友们，你们逼我做的事，偏偏是我从来都不想做的事情。你们想一想，娶一位和自己志趣相投的妻子有多困难，而娶一个跟自己合不来的女

1. 原标题为"第十天第十则故事"。

人却是大有可能。要是娶了这么一个女人，日子该多不好过啊！你们真蠢，竟然以为，只要摸清姑娘父母的品性，就能找到让我满意的妻子。我不知道你们如何认识了她们父亲，也不知道你们如何窥探到了她们母亲的隐私。就算你们明白了姑娘父母的情况，又怎么保证她和父母一模一样呢？但既然你们执意要给我套上这道枷锁，我只能欣然接受。不过，我要自己选择妻子。就算之后事情进展得不顺利，我也用不着怪罪别人。我还要告诉你们，不管我最后选了谁，你们都要尊敬她。要是我按照你们的意愿，娶了一个自己不喜欢的女人，那我有多不爽快，就会让你们吃到多大的苦头。”他那些精明的手下立刻回答说，只要侯爵肯娶亲，无论娶谁，他们都会高兴的。

在附近的村子里，住着一个出身贫寒的姑娘。侯爵欣赏她的品性已经有很长一段时日了。而且他也十分欣赏姑娘的美貌，觉得与她一起生活应该会很开心。于是他就不再物色别人，直接挑明要娶她。侯爵派人把姑娘的父亲叫了过来，向他表明了心意。姑娘的父亲十分贫穷，所以立刻答应了这门婚事。

办完这些事后，瓜尔蒂耶里侯爵把辖区内所有的居

民都召集过来，对他们说："朋友们，我知道你们很想让我娶亲，我也马上就要结婚了。但我成亲，多半是为了让你们开心，并非我自己所想。你们答应过我，无论我娶谁回家都会同意，而且都会尊敬她。现在，是时候让我来履行我对你们许下的诺言，也是时候让你们兑现承诺了。我按照自己的心愿找到了附近的一位姑娘，不日就会和她在府里成婚。所以，你们要想一想，该如何办一场热闹的婚礼，又该如何迎娶她。这样一来，你们让我高兴，我也会让你们满意。"

大家听到这个消息后都很兴奋，回答说，无论侯爵想要娶谁，他们都会欣然接受，并且在任何时候都会尊敬她，视她为自己的女主人。那之后，大伙很快就投入到这一庆典的准备当中，瓜尔蒂耶里本人也参与了筹备过程。侯爵让他们把婚礼办得豪华隆重，还邀请了所有亲朋好友以及周边地区的上层人士来参加庆典。此外，他还找来了一位与新娘身材差不多的姑娘，按照她的尺寸做了很多华丽的衣服，又置办了几条腰带、一枚戒指和一顶漂亮的王冠。总之，只要是新嫁娘会用到的东西，他都准备好了。

到了婚礼那天，瓜尔蒂耶里一大早就上了马，要和

他一起迎娶新娘的人也都到齐了。一切安排妥当后，手下人对侯爵说：“大人，是时候去接新娘了。”于是，侯爵在其他人的陪同下，朝着那个小村子出发了。到了之后，他们看到姑娘抬着刚从井里打来的水，急急忙忙地往家赶，周围还有几个同行的姑娘，大概是为了来看一眼侯爵的新娘。瓜尔蒂耶里看到她后，知道她名叫格里塞尔达，就叫了她一声，问她父亲在哪里。姑娘羞答答地回答道：“大人，他在家里呢。”

于是瓜尔蒂耶里下了马，让众人在外面等着，自己一个人走进了那个简陋的房子。见到姑娘的父亲贾努科雷后，侯爵对他说：“我来娶格里塞尔达回府，但是在此之前，我想当着你的面问她几个问题。”于是侯爵问格里塞尔达，结婚之后不管自己说什么话，做什么事，她会不会始终顺从于他，讨好于他。姑娘回答“会”。他又问了很多诸如此类的问题，格里塞尔达都做出了肯定的回答。

听到格里塞尔达的回答后，侯爵便牵起了她的手，把她带到了屋外，吩咐手下的人将她的旧衣裳脱掉，换上他备好的华服。很快，他们就打扮好了新娘，还梳理了她原本蓬乱的头发，为她戴上了王冠。在场的每一个人都为这一幕惊叹不已。于是侯爵说：“诸位，只要这位

姑娘同意，她就是我要娶的妻子了。”接着他转过身来问姑娘：“格里塞尔达，你愿意让我做你的丈夫吗？”

格里塞尔达还是那么羞涩，不敢相信这是真的，怯生生地回答道：“大人，我愿意。”

于是侯爵说：“我也愿意让你做我的妻子。”就这样，侯爵在所有人的见证下娶走了她。他将她扶上一匹小马，风风光光地回了侯爵府。在府里，他们举行了盛大的仪式。就算是法国公主出嫁，也不过如此了。

换上新衣服后，年轻的新娘就像变了个人似的。我们刚才说过，她本就貌美如花，温柔贤淑，再经过这么一番打扮，就更加惹人喜爱了。现在的她宛若一位大家闺秀、贵族小姐，根本不像是农民贾努科雷的女儿，更不像是个放羊的姑娘了，这让之前认识她的人都惊讶万分。而且她对丈夫也十分恭顺，时刻让他感到自己是世界上最快乐、最有福气的男人。除此之外，她对丈夫手下的人也非常和蔼宽厚。每个人都衷心地爱戴她，尊敬她，祈祷她身体健康，事事顺意。有些人之前说瓜尔蒂耶里娶这个女人是犯了糊涂，现在就连他们也说，瓜尔蒂耶里料事如神，是天下最聪明的男人，因为再也没有人能像他一样，透过乡下女子的粗布衣衫，窥探到如此

高尚的品德。不久，格里塞尔达的名声不仅传遍了整个侯爵领地，还传到了其他各个地方。她证明了自己的价值和品德，也让之前反对侯爵娶她的人改变了主意。

和瓜尔蒂耶里一起住了没多久后，格里塞尔达就怀孕了。几个月后，一个女婴呱呱坠地。瓜尔蒂耶里十分高兴，然而没过多长时间，他心里就萌生了一个奇怪的念头。他想用一些常人无法忍受的事考验妻子的耐心，而且要考验她很长时间。瓜尔蒂耶里先是用语言打击她。他装出心神不宁的样子，对夫人说因为她出身寒微，所以下属们对她很不满意。特别是当她生孩子时，大家一看是个女孩，都很不高兴，一直在嘀咕。

听到这些话后，夫人镇定自若，连一点多余的举动都没有。她说："大人，您想对我做什么就做什么吧。只要能对您的名誉有利，能令您高兴，那您对我做什么，我都会心甘情愿地接受。我知道，我没有您的下属重要，而且我本就配不上您对我的尊重。"这个回答很合瓜尔蒂耶里的心意，因为他从这些话里听出，妻子并没有因为自己和他人的尊敬而骄傲自大。

没过多长时间，瓜尔蒂耶里又向妻子暗示，下属们容不下她生的这个女儿。然后，他又叫来府上一个仆人，

派他去夫人那里做件事。到了格里塞尔达面前，仆人面露难色地对她说："夫人，我要是不按大人吩咐的做，大人就会杀了我的。他让我把您的女儿带走，让我……"他说到这里，就没再说下去了。

格里塞尔达听了这话，再看看这个仆人的脸色，想起侯爵之前说的话，便明白了丈夫是派他来杀女儿的。尽管心里悲恸欲绝，但她仍然面不改色，立刻把女儿从摇篮里抱了起来，在一番亲吻、祝福之后，把孩子给了仆人，对他说："带她走吧！既然你的主人要你这么做，那你按他的命令照做就是了。但请你别让鸟兽吃掉孩子的尸身，除非大人命令你必须这么做。"仆人抱着孩子，把夫人说的话重复给了侯爵听。妻子坚强的意志让他感到十分惊讶，于是，他把女儿送到了博洛尼亚的一位亲戚那里，请亲戚悉心照料教导她，但永远不要让孩子知道自己的身世。

不久，夫人又怀孕了，这次生下了一名男婴。瓜尔蒂耶里十分喜欢这个孩子，但觉得之前做的还不够，想用更大的打击来考验妻子。一天，他又装作心绪不定的样子对妻子说："夫人，自从你生了这个儿子，我手下那些人知道我死以后，贾努科雷的外孙要做他们的主公，

就一直闹得不可开交。我实在受不了他们了。要想不被他们推翻，我恐怕还得再对儿子做一次上次对女儿做的事情，不然最后还得离开你，再娶一个女人。”妻子耐心地听他讲完，只是回答说：“大人，请您按自己的意愿行事。您只管让自己开心就好，不用考虑我。因为如果看到您不开心，我做什么事情都不会开心的。”

没过几天，瓜尔蒂耶里又像当年送走女儿一样，送走了儿子。和上次一样，他假装把孩子杀掉，但其实还是送到了博洛尼亚抚养。而夫人也和上次送走女儿时一样，没流露出一丝多余的神情，也没说一句多余的话。瓜尔蒂耶里看到后震惊了，越发确信没有女人可以做到她这般隐忍。如果不是亲眼看到格里塞尔达与自己一样疼爱孩子的话，他还以为妻子根本没把孩子放在心上呢。而格里塞尔达也很聪明，让丈夫看出了自己对孩子的爱。侯爵的下属们以为他真的把两个孩子杀了，于是都强烈地谴责他，觉得他是个残忍无情的人，也都对夫人表现出了极大的同情。别人家的夫人看她失去了孩子，过来安慰她。但她只是说，如果孩子的亲生父亲想这么做，那么她也愿意这么做。

女儿长大后，瓜尔蒂耶里觉得考验妻子忍耐力的最

终时刻到了。当着众多下属的面，瓜尔蒂耶里宣称，他再也忍受不了夫人了，还说当初娶她是因为年少无知，所以想请求教皇特许，让他离开格里塞尔达，再娶新人。很多下属反对他，但他却说自己只能这么做。夫人听说这件事后，想到自己要回娘家，像从前那样终日放羊，还要看着另一个女人与自己心爱的丈夫在一起生活，心里十分难过。然而，就像以前接受不公的命运时一样，这次她仍然隐忍不发，听从命运的安排。

没过多久，瓜尔蒂耶里就派人从罗马寄回几封伪造的信，让手下的人看到，教皇已经在信中特许他休掉格里塞尔达，另娶他人。接着，他派人把格里塞尔达叫来，当着众人的面对她说："夫人，我获得了教皇的特许，可以把你休掉再娶了。我的祖上都是这里的达官贵人，而你家世世代代都是农民，所以我不想让你做我的妻子了，但你可以带着嫁妆回贾努科雷家。我也已经找到了一位适合我的妻子，过几天就会把她娶来。"

夫人听到这些话后，费了好大的劲才克制住女人的天性，把眼泪咽到肚子里，回答道："大人，我知道自己出身卑微，配不上高贵的您。多亏了上帝的恩赐和您的宠爱，我才能和您在一起。尽管您给了我尊位，但我始

终不敢把自己当成侯爵夫人，只觉得自己沾了您的光。既然您想收回送给我的东西，那么我也愿意将它们还给您。这是您娶我时用的戒指，请您收下吧。至于您让我把带过来的嫁妆带走，这既不用您花钱找人来搬，也不用我叫牲口来驮，因为我还没有忘记，我嫁给您时，什么也没有带过来，连身上穿的衣服都是您给的。如果您觉得可行的话，我也可以赤裸着走出去，让大家都看看我这为您生了两个孩子的身子。但我是带着童贞过来的，现在已经带不走了，所以我求求您看在这分儿上，除了本就不存在的嫁妆之外，至少让我再穿走一件衣服吧。”

瓜尔蒂耶里感动得直想哭，但仍然板着脸说：“那你就穿件衣服吧。”

周围的人都求侯爵再给夫人件衣裳，别让相伴十三年的妻子只穿一件内衣，走得那么寒酸，那么不光彩。但他们怎么求侯爵都没有用，夫人还是辞别了众人，摘去头饰，身穿一件单衣，赤足走出了侯爵府，回到了父亲家。所有看到这一幕的人无不痛哭流涕。而贾努科雷从未相信过瓜尔蒂耶里是真心实意要娶女儿为妻，所以每时每刻都在等待这一天的到来。他还一直留着瓜尔蒂耶里娶亲时，女儿脱下来的衣服，等女儿回娘家时再给

她继续穿。回家后，格里塞尔达还是像之前一样干些杂务活。尽管命运多舛，她还是凭借顽强的意志忍耐了下来。

瓜尔蒂耶里做完这些事后，便对他手下的人说，自己看中了帕纳戈一位公爵的女儿，让他们好好筹备婚礼，又派人把格里塞尔达叫来。格里塞尔达到了后，侯爵对她说:“我新看中了一个姑娘，想让她第一次进我家门时风光一番。你知道，办这么一场婚礼，需要有人收拾屋子，处理许多杂务，而我府上没有一个女佣能担得起这差事。你比其他任何人都熟悉这些事务，所以我派你来主持工作。除此之外，你还要把这附近该邀请的太太都请过来，最后像迎接女主人一样，迎接我的新婚妻子。办完这些事后，你就可以回娘家了。”

这些话就像刀子一样扎在格里塞尔达心上。曾经的好运让她拥有了深爱丈夫的权利，现在她已然失去了这份权利，但实在不忍心割舍这份感情。然而，她只是回答说:“大人，我准备好了。”于是她穿着粗布衣衫，又走进了那座不久前身穿单衣离开的府第，开始布置房间。她在床头挂上装饰品，给客厅铺好地毯，又收拾了厨房。事无巨细，她都亲自动手，就像一个卑贱的女佣。直到把所有东西都布置妥当，又以侯爵的名义邀请完附近府

上的夫人之后，她才停下歇了歇，等待婚礼的到来。到了婚礼那天，她面带笑容，迎接了所有的女宾。尽管穿着破衣旧衫，但她举止大方，谈吐得体，如同一位贵族夫人。

侯爵之前把孩子送给了博洛尼亚的亲戚抚养，而亲戚的丈夫正是帕纳戈的伯爵。现在，瓜尔蒂耶里和格里塞尔达的女儿已经长到了十二岁，出落得亭亭玉立，宛若仙女一般。他们的儿子也已经六岁了。瓜尔蒂耶里写信给亲戚，请他把女儿和儿子送回桑卢佐，还拜托他派阵势浩大的随从护送他们，告诉所有人，女儿将会嫁给瓜尔蒂耶里侯爵，但不要告诉任何人她的真实身份。这位亲戚按照侯爵的请求一一照做，带着姑娘、弟弟和随从们出发了。几天后，他们在午餐时分到达了桑卢佐。当地所有村民，以及附近村子里的人都在桑卢佐等候瓜尔蒂耶里侯爵的新娘。女宾们把姑娘迎到了府上，而在布好筵席的客厅里，格里塞尔达像往常一样，兴高采烈地迎上去说:“欢迎夫人！”其实女宾们早就求瓜尔蒂耶里，让格里塞尔达待在另一个房间里，或者给她些衣物，别让她在客人面前出这么大的丑，但瓜尔蒂耶里不答应。这时，她们只好就座，等待婚礼开始。每个人看了那姑

娘后，都说瓜尔蒂耶里换夫人换得好，格里塞尔达也对姑娘和她弟弟赞不绝口。

瓜尔蒂耶里看到所有这些场景，觉得对夫人耐心的考验已经足够了。他看到格里塞尔达从不改变态度，始终恭顺谦卑，又知道她很聪慧，并不是由于智力缺陷才会如此，所以认为是时候解除她所有的痛苦了。他还知道，尽管她没有把这些痛苦表现在脸上，但一定藏在了心里。于是，瓜尔蒂耶里把格里塞尔达叫来，当着所有人的面，微笑着问她：“你觉得我的新娘怎么样？”

“大人”，格里塞尔达回答说，“我觉得她非常好，既美丽又聪慧。我觉得，您和她一起生活，一定会成为世上最快乐的人。但我求求您，不要像对待您上一位妻子一样对待她，叫她受到那么多伤害。您的前妻自小就饱受苦难，所以并无大碍；而她一向被娇生惯养，是忍受不了这些挫折的。”

瓜尔蒂耶里看到格里塞尔达如此坚信自己会娶这姑娘为妻，而且没有一句抱怨的话，于是让她坐在自己身边，对她说：“格里塞尔达，你忍耐了这么长时间，是时候让你得到回报，也是时候让那些说我残酷不义的人知道我这么做的目的了。我之所以这么做，是想要教会你

该如何做一个妻子，并且让大家知道该如何对待我的妻子，好让我们的生活永远平安顺利。刚娶你时，我非常害怕你会不听我的话，所以才想方设法地试探你，甚至伤害你。然而，你说的每句话都顺我的心，做的每件事都合我的意。我觉得拥有你，就等于拥有了我期盼的所有宽慰和欣喜。现在，我想一次性弥补之前对你的亏欠，用我全部的温柔抚慰你受伤的心。来，高高兴兴地牵起这姑娘和这男孩的手吧，因为你相信我要娶的这位姑娘就是我们的女儿，而这男孩就是我们的儿子。他们两人就是你们以为被我残忍杀害的孩子。而我，是你的丈夫，我爱你胜过世间万物。我相信，现在我可以自豪地说，没有人能够像我一样，对自己的妻子如此满意。”

说罢，他拥吻了妻子。格里塞尔达喜极而泣，和丈夫一起站起来，向女儿走去。他们的女儿听完这些事情后又惊又喜，在场的众人到这时也才明白了侯爵的所作所为。格里塞尔达温柔地拥抱了女儿，又抱住了儿子。女宾们也非常欣慰，纷纷起身祝贺格里塞尔达，然后和她去里间，帮她脱下了那身粗布衣裳，换上了一身她之前穿的华服，将女主人迎回客厅。其实，就算穿着方才那身衣服，她看起来仍像是府上的女主人。格里塞尔达

和孩子们都欣喜若狂，大家也都兴奋不已，于是一连庆祝了好几天。大家虽然觉得瓜尔蒂耶里对妻子做的事不近人情，但都夸他聪明绝顶，对格里塞尔达的智慧更是赞不绝口。

几天后，帕纳戈伯爵回到了博洛尼亚。瓜尔蒂耶里也把丈人贾努科雷接到了府里，让他不必再劳累度日，以安享晚年。他又把自己和格里塞尔达的女儿嫁给了一个富贵人家，而他自己则和格里塞尔达幸福地生活了一辈子。

现在，我们能说什么呢？高尚的灵魂也会降临到穷人家里，正如一些为人主公的贵族子弟只配去喂猪一样。除了格里塞尔达以外，还有谁能像她一样，在自己的丈夫做了那些残忍无比的事情后，不仅可以忍住不哭，还能面带笑意呢？如果换成另一个女人穿着单衣，被瓜尔蒂耶里赶出家门的话，那她就会去找别的男人，让他再给自己一身漂亮的新衣服。这听起来好像也没什么不对的。

PENGUIN

LITTLE BLACK

CLASSICS